PASSENGER TO PENZANCE

By the same author:
Short Stories:
    The Secret Place
    Echoes from the Cornish Cliffs
    A Summer to Remember

Autobiographical:
    The Wind Blows from the West
    A Long Way to Land's End
    A View from the Valley
    Sunset over the Scillies
    Spring at Land's End
    An Old Mill by the Stream
    The Petrified Mariner

Passenger to Penzance

and other stories

by

Denys Val Baker

WILLIAM KIMBER · LONDON

First published in 1978 by
WILLIAM KIMBER & CO. LIMITED
Godolphin House, 22a Queen Anne's Gate,
London, SW1H 9AE

© Denys Val Baker, 1978

ISBN 0 7183 0465 9

This book is copyright. No part of it may be reproduced in any form without permission in writing from the publishers except by a reviewer who wishes to quote brief passages in connection with a review written for inclusion in a newspaper, magazine or radio broadcast.

Photoset in Great Britain by
Specialised Offset Services Limited, Liverpool
and printed by
REDWOOD BURN LIMITED
Trowbridge & Esher

Contents

		Page
I	The Sailor's Return	7
II	The Face in the Mirror	36
III	The Happiest Day of Their Lives	50
IV	The Woman Who Walked Away	59
V	The Surfer	74
VI	A Man and a Trumpet	81
VII	A Literary Letter	97
VIII	Like Summertime	106
IX	Passenger to Penzance	117
X	The Last Day	125
XI	The Woman on the Couch	134
XII	A Rose In Winter	145
XIII	The Man They'll Mourn in Vain	169

I
The Sailor's Return

When I was a boy I used to spend the summer holidays staying with my Aunty Mags Johnson and her two children, Mark and Betty, at her big red brick boarding house on the front at Penporth, which is somewhere along the bottom corner of Cornwall. At one time the house had been the summer residence of a Lancashire cotton merchant and his family, but ever since I could remember it wore a yellow board over the porch: 'Private Boarding Establishment. Proprietress, Mrs Mags Johnson.'

I have a clear picture of my Aunty Mags as she was then, a small, neat woman with grey hair done up in a fluffy bun and a pair of gold rimmed spectacles perched on her nose when she remembered about them: not the sort of person to make you stop and look twice, though if you had troubled you might have been pleasantly rewarded, for she had been quite a beauty in her day.

Most of the time Aunty Mags went about in a fussy, harassed manner, for it must have been no joke coping with a dozen or more boarders, four meals a day, not to mention the children. But occasionally you might catch Aunty Mags off guard, leaning out of a window or staring into the fire, and then there was a surprising softness of her face, and in the bright brown eyes a wistful reflection of earlier beauty. Then, you could have safely bet yourself, Aunty Mags was thinking sentimentally about her husband, my Uncle Walter, and their unknown life together before he had packed his things into an old black sack and gone away to sea. We gathered from Aunty Mags that Uncle Walter had tried his very hardest to settle down to a land-bound life but that, coming as he did from a long line of sea-faring men, it would have been going against nature for him to have resisted the call of the sea.

In her heart of hearts Aunty Mags was really a very sentimental person, and for all her undoubted bouts of loneliness she had found something rather romantic in Uncle Walter's melodramatic departure, and the idea of his restless sailing of the world's seas. Over the years material circumstances had caused her to set up in business on her own – and a very successful business, too. But she had continued to enjoy the company, if not of Uncle Walter's person, of his romantic legend, growing more romantic and colourful with each year's passage. Sometimes a neighbour might be overheard speaking unkindly about Uncle Walter's travels that kept him so long from home, but if we told Aunty Mags she always turned up her nose angrily and said that we should mind our own business like certain others should mind theirs, too.

Uncle Walter had been roaming the seas a good many years, so I had never met him, but there were always reports of his travels, as well as periodical rumours of his impending return. Every time I went to stay at Penporth the first thing I did – after stuffing myself with one of Aunty Mags' special teas of gold-buttered fruit-bread and dark red strawberry jam, with hot shortbreads to follow – was to draw Mark and Betty aside and demand, 'Has she had any news from – you-know-who?'

Then three heads would bend conspiratorially nearer until we formed a closed circle of great secrets. Betty would hiss out her breath, nervously, and Mark, black eyes dancing with fun, would run his tongue around his lips and whisper, 'Yes, Mam still hears about once a month – and what do you think? Dad's been to America and stayed in New York and San Francisco and Hollywood – oh, and lots and lots of places. And where do you think he's just been to? Why, he's been to Honolulu! Fancy that!' – his eyes glowing bigger and bigger with wonder.

But Betty would often frown, pouting, and say, 'I don't

think once every month is enough, do you, David?' – and the way she said it, so serious and disapproving, we all felt a little frightened, as if, beneath all the excitement, we were glimpsing a revelation of something sad and hurtful.

Most of the time Aunty Mags went through life – bustling about the house, tidying up here and straightening out there, a cheery, fussy little figure – as if there was no such person as Uncle Walter, as if she had no great secret of a link across the world. But there were some days when the postman gave an extra loud rap on the door to show that he had an important letter, and then you would hear Aunty Mags' footsteps scurrying down the stairs so that she would be the first to see the postman. By the time anyone else got near the letters the most interesting one of all was gone, safely tucked away in Aunty Mags' apron pocket for reading in the quiet of her own room. What a lot of exciting tales there must have been in those letters, we used to think, enviously – how we longed to be able to read right through from beginning to end, even just one letter. Of course, we never got that opportunity.

On the other hand, Aunty Mags would have burst if she had had to bottle up all her excitement after receiving a letter, and so she would condescend to read short, carefully selected extracts. Those were cosy occasions indeed! The three of us squatting round the fire of Aunty Mags' sitting-room in the evening, when at long last the worry of attending her guests was ended for another day. If it turned cool Aunty Mags would build up a cheerful fire out of dried wood collected off the beach, and by the light of this she would read little passages from Uncle Walter's large scraggly handwriting.

What Aunty Mags read out did not seem to me, even at that time, quite worthy of all the fuss and excitement, and yet by the way she read – her voice warm and low, half-singing the words – you knew what a lot the letter meant in her life. Perhaps it did not matter what words Uncle Walter happened to write, only that he wrote at all? And no one could deny, I thought, that a letter coming all that long way meant some sort of a link in the chain binding two people.

The summer I am thinking about was hotter than usual.

There had been none of the usual summer storms stealing up from behind the moors, only the same dazzling blue sky and the same scorching sun frying us brown as berries. Mark and Betty and I spent the best part of our time lazing on the warm sands, while the crooked tide crept in and then out again, always guarded over by chattering seagulls and puffins on the look out for an extra meal.

In the mornings we used to take a stick and a rubber ball and play exciting games of rounders with some of the other children, cooling off afterwards with a swift splash in the glittering sea. In the afternoons we might stir ourselves to go to the edge of the beach and wave enthusiastically at one of the fat pleasure boats from St Ives packed with gaily coloured holiday trippers. At night, as often as not, we would walk out along the rock-strewn headland, because from the tip of this we could watch the sun setting the sky on fire as it died across the other side of the bay ... When that ritual was over we could shift our gaze and stare out seawards, for there the sky took on a mystic phosphorescent radiance, delicately illuminated by the last desperate slanting rays of light, and out of the growing dusk we could catch the winking of the western lighthouse, or perhaps even of a distant ship.

Betty, I remember, had a peaceful way of looking; bright gold head cocked to one side and plump body standing firm and straight as though she was content just to accept the beauty and wonder of the rainbow-dyed view. But Mark's was a restless stare, having no eye for beauties of sky or view, concerned only with the great, glowing sheet of green sea, and any possible indication of a ship passing its self-contained way through the night and the lonely ocean.

Mark was fascinated with ships and the idea of sailing on and on across some endless swishing world of water. Already he lived largely in an imaginary world of water and steamboats and sailing boats, of bosuns and mates and captains, and cabin boys, too. He was always asking nautical questions of Mr Stevens, who ran motor boat trips across the bay at a shilling a time. At home Mark's interest in the sea was often sharply discouraged by Aunty Mags, so when we were away from that restraint Mark used to make up for lost time by regaling me with streams of half-digested information which he had acquired from various sources. He was a determined, persuasive sort of boy, Mark, good-looking and impressive with his curly black hair and alive, questing eyes.

Sometimes he would talk me into sharing his exhilarating bursts of enthusiasm, his wistful, as yet not quite clarified ambitions. But other times I would find myself remembering the grey background of mainland and moors, behind us, filling half the sky with their crooked spouts and blunted shoulders – how their vast shape dwarfed the steamers and all their proud red funnels – and brought even the great sea to an end. But Mark never looked anywhere except out to sea and he laughed at my silly thoughts.

One afternoon, when Betty was helping her mother with the housework, Mark and I borrowed two old tea trays and climbed up to the top of a sharp hill just outside the village. From there we could enjoy the thrills of tray-skiing full pelt down the hundred foot slope. When at last we were tired we climbed to the top for the last time and threw ourselves down, exhausted, lying side by side with our hands over our heads to shade away the sun.

Suddenly Mark raised himself on his elbows, peering out to sea, flat blue below us. His sharp face was screwed up with the intensity of the effort.

'What is it?' I asked.

Mark pointed excitedly.

'Look, ships! – one, two – *three* of them!'

With some difficulty I traced the smoke patches curling against the horizon. I don't suppose I would have noticed them on my own: they were so far away, seemed so remote and unreal.

'Where will they be going?' I asked, dropping my eyes at last to relieve the strain.

'Oooh! – anywhere, everywhere,' said Mark, still staring. His eyes sparkled with sudden vitality. 'Maybe they're passenger boats bound for Ireland, or perhaps New York. Old Man Stevens says those are the biggest ships he's ever seen.

And he should know!'

'Yes,' I said, thinking of old Mr Stevens who would even now be sitting impassively on the edge of his jetway, smoking his old pipe and watching the children paddling about at the edge of the sands, occasionally calling out in a grumbly tone for them to keep clear of the break-water.

'Fancy,' said Mark, 'the people aboard might be going to the other end of the world. America, Canada, Australia – Rio de Janeiro, the Panama Canal ...' He began reeling off the names. 'Think of it, David, seeing all those places ... There they go, and here we are on a silly hill-top!'

He paused.

'Funny to think of our Dad out there,' he went on thoughtfully. And then fell silent again.

'There they go,' he said, as the streaks of smoke began fading.

'Shall we be getting back?' I said.

'Yes.'

We got to our feet and picked up the trays.

'Final race!' cried Mark. He took a last look out to sea.

'Funny, you know,' he said again, 'to think of our Dad out there. I'll bet he's seen some wonderful sights!'

'I'll bet he has,' I said.

'More than you'll ever see at Penporth, sitting on a silly old hill!' said Mark crossly, and there was a most curious inflection to his voice. Then:

'Ready-steady-go!' he cried out.

And away we went, slithering down the smooth green hillside, jerking from side to side, in and out of the prickly gorse bushes. I with my heart in my mouth and thinking every bush ahead would be the end of me – but Mark poking ahead, lying almost flat down with his hair blowing all over the place and the gleam of excitement in his eyes, so that you felt then there was nothing he wouldn't do if he had set his heart on it, no matter how long he had to wait.

It was when we got back that afternoon, hungry for our tea, that we were met along the front by Betty, running towards us with her hair blowing wild and an altogether topsy-turvy appearance about her usual demure self.

'What do you think? What do you think?' she said excitedly. 'Dad is coming home. Really and truly, Mam has had a letter – an *air mail letter*!'

The fact that Uncle Walter had seen fit to expend whatever enormous extra money was required for air mailing a letter was obviously proof enough that something dramatic was in the wind.

'Really?' whistled Mark, his eyes brightening. 'Coming home – here?'

We ran back, up the steps and through the hallway into the kitchen, where Aunty Mags was getting the boarders' supper ready.

'Is it true about Dad?' cried Mark excitedly, dancing around his mother.

Aunty Mags attempted to look unconcerned, but she of all people was the last to be able to hide that look in her eyes. In any case she was too full of her news to be able to bottle it up.

'So your Dad says,' she admitted. She felt into her bosom for a crumpled letter and brought it out to read us – as much of it as she considered fit for our ears.

Holding it at arm's length, because of her short sight, she picked out the news.

'He says he's on his way home, making his last trip – his *last* trip, mind you – and as soon as he gets here he's handing in his books and retiring. Would you ever, our Dad retiring from the sea!' She rolled her eyes round disbelievingly. 'Believe that when we see it, eh?' she said skittishly. But even then, young as I was, I fancied I sensed something behind the bantering, sensed the pathetic desire really to believe the news without any qualification.

'Where did the letter come from?' demanded Mark impatiently. 'And can I have the stamp please?' he added practically.

Aunty Mags screwed her eyes up.

'B-U-E-N-O-S-A-I-R-E-S,' she spelt out slowly. 'Heaven knows where that is, though.'

'It's in Argentina,' explained Mark pityingly, his eyes

gleaming he did a quick reckoning of distances, knots per hour, and so on. 'Mmmmh ...' His head sank lower and lower under the strain. At last it tossed up triumphantly.

'Sixteen days and our Dad should be back in Britain,' he said. 'Here, let me see the postmark.' He whistled. 'He might even be back already!'

Aunty Mags screamed in mock alarm.

'What! I haven't even started to get ready. Here, out you go, all of you – your tea's out in the front room. Now let me be.'

It was like that for the rest of the days before Uncle Walter arrived. The boarders, myself, Mark and Betty, we all got scant shrift from Aunty Mags, and she was equally impartial in her tellings-off for anyone or anything likely to hold up her immense preparations. However, everyone was really quite as thrilled about the news as Aunty Mags, and allowance was readily made for all her whims and caprices.

Now, in addition to all her ordinary work, she embarked on vast rearrangements of rooms and accommodation. Poor Aunty Mags, usually so active and masterful – and there she was, suddenly as fluttery and clucky as a helpless old lady. First she decided that she and Uncle Walter would occupy the front bedroom on the second floor, since it was the biggest in the house, with a fine view over the sea. Then, after she had wheedled Mr and Mrs Dennison into packing their things and moving out of there into another room, she remembered that Uncle Walter was worried by heights and decided he might not be able to sleep as high as the second floor. So she decided in favour of the front room on the first floor, and accordingly turned out a young couple from Manchester after their first night there. Even then she could not rest contented.

In the end she fixed on a ground-floor room as Uncle Walter's abode-to-be. We were all called in to spend a heavy morning re-arranging furniture and cleaning the room out – though needless to say Aunty Mags went all over it again with duster and polish as soon as we had finished. The front room it was to be then; for the present. 'If your Dad doesn't like it we can soon move up to the first-floor one, can't we?' said

Aunty Mags reflectively, raising one more of the many shadowy clouds of pessimism that she seemed to create in the midst of all her supposedly joyful preparations.

Sometimes I used to wonder about this curious suggestion of pessimism. It never seemed to strike Mark and Betty who, fairly naturally, had given themselves up entirely to the drama unfolding before them, with its eagerly awaited happy ending. I decided I was imagining things and ought to stop wondering. But another day, when I was out shopping with Betty in the high street, the piping voice of Mrs Tonkins, a neighbouring boarding-house keeper, cut across my hearing. She was talking in that confiding way so beloved of most of the local housewives, to Mrs Richards the fishmonger's wife. I heard her mention Mrs Johnson and I knew she meant Aunty Mags. Besides she prefixed the name with the adjective 'poor'. And then she said, emphatically:

'It won't be easy, you know. It won't be easy, Mrs Richards. Just you imagine, Mrs Richards, if your Mr Richards or my Mr Tonkins had been away all that time – and then they came back, just like that. Oh, my, what a game it would be! It wouldn't be as simple as it sounds, Mrs Richards. But Mrs Johnson, she's gone silly, she doesn't think about anything if you ask me, now. Why, I was saying to her the other day – what's he going to do …?'

Then Betty came out of the next-door greengrocer's shop, her basket full of long green beans and some lettuce and a parcel of gold-brown plums, and we moved on.

'Old windbag, Mrs Tonkins,' she sniffed, when I told her. But I noticed on reflection, that she did not directly oppose Mrs Tonkins' views.

I felt that Mrs Tonkins was wrong in her estimate of Aunty Mags' inability to look ahead: but that was just the trouble. As the day drew nearer I took to watching Aunty Mags closely, with the morbid fascination of an inquisitive and impressionable boy. And the more I watched the more I had a strange sensation, something like you might have when watching one of those trick stage dancers who looks as if he is walking forward – and all the time he is really not moving at all, or even retreating. Or like that, if you see my meaning.

But what a day it was when Uncle Walter did arrive! He came on the afternoon express, and at first we planned a triumphal reception at the station. Mark even suggested, quite seriously, that Betty should take a bouquet of flowers. But in the end Aunty Mags, after being so excited that she was nearly hysterical, became quite calm again and said, No, she would prefer to go on her own. The rest of us could be waiting at the gate to welcome them both back when they drew up in Mr Pengelly's taxi, which had been hired for days beforehand for the occasion.

Oh, you should have seen my Aunty Mags that day! She had bought herself a new summer dress specially for the occasion – bright sea-blue it was, blowing about her prettily in the breeze – and she had smart, high-heeled shoes and silk stockings and spotless white gloves on her hands. To finish it all off, there was a new hat she had gone all the way to Plymouth to buy; rather a flappery hat, I suppose it was, but there it was perched on my Aunty Mags' head, with a cluster of cream and crimson flowers at the front and a thin black strap holding it on at the back. She held herself proud and lovely that day, my Aunty Mags, as she set off walking along the promenade to the station, a good hour before the train was due – and nothing she had for lunch but a strong cup of tea. Happy and joyful she must have been that day, yet I've often fancied since that you might have seen the strangest things if you had been able to look really deep into her eyes.

Exactly what took place when Uncle Walter's train arrived, whether they fell into each other's arms like in the story books, I've never rightly known – though we were all of us speculating about it after the train had rumbled by on the gradient higher up outside the village, and as we heard its brakes clapped on approaching the station. Anyway the long-drawn minutes went by and at last we saw the taxi turn on to the prom and come ambling along, as if all the world had time to spare – and I suppose there really wasn't any need for hurry. When the taxi drew up outside we all crowded round the gate. Aunty Mags stepped out all of a fluster, and then behind her came a little dark-eyed man wearing a rather bright check suit; a huge new bowler hat towering above his head, his face white with nervousness, and his thick blue-tattooed hands twisting to indicate his embarrassment. Uncle Walter was home.

'Oh, dearie me, oh dearie me!' exclaimed Aunty Mags, breathlessly, while Uncle Walter dutifully paid Mr Pengelly. Then, rather obviously, she exclaimed:

'Mark! Betty! Here's your Dad!' And there was a flurry of kisses and backslaps and offers of help to carry the suitcases and a lot of laughing and then, after I had been introduced as London Cousin David, we made a slow, untidy way up the path into the cool of the house.

'Well, well,' said Uncle Walter, as we came to the porch, looking from Mark to Betty and Betty to Mark, 'How you've grown, you two ... Last time I saw you you were so high!' – and he held his hand down below the level of his knee.

Then, feeling that perhaps it had not been a very happy remark to make, he straightened up again awkwardly. But you could see that the first agony was over, some of the white was going and the tell-tale brown of faraway suns coming through again. And sure enough, it wasn't long before Uncle Walter had recovered, mellowing under the showers of attention heaped upon him. You could see that he was beginning to enjoy himself, as we sat laughing and talking in the sitting-room.

'Like to fetch my old kit-bag, Mark boy?' he said jovially, glimmers of all sorts of exciting promises in his eyes. Mark scampered into the hall to drag in the bag, bulky with mysterious packages.

And then it was a time of fancy presents and colourful gifts from colourful lands; strings of coral pearls, a piece of precious amber shell, a rust-coloured Javanese ivory back-scratcher, strange wooden carvings from India, little Japanese painted masks, a crimson Mexican scarf (a special present for Aunty Mags, that) and some real Spanish oranges and a bunch of huge Portuguese bananas which Uncle Walter picked up on the trip back. For Betty there were some pearls, and a present was found for me in the form of a brass dagger which Uncle Walter assured me was carved by a Siamese tribal chief.

But the showpiece of all was undoubtedly Mark's present – none other than a beautiful and intricately fashioned model of an old sailing ship. When Uncle Walter carefully unwrapped its sheets of paper covering and exposed it in all its glory, we all echoed Mark's whistle of wonder. The ship had been carved out of a smooth teak wood and painted all over a sheer white; the rigging and tiny deck rails were all steely silver, with bright red lanterns hung here and there, so that there was an impression of light and freshness everywhere. Not only was there a tiny figurehead, a carved horse's head, but there were all the rows of sails after the fashion of one of the old wind-jammers.

'Made out of real sail cloth they were, too,' commented Uncle Walter proudly. 'I made it on the trip home. Took me most of the time, I can tell you.' He had been watching Mark closely for his reactions, and he looked pleased at the continued expression of awe and envy.

'It's all yours, my boy,' he said cheerfully, patting Mark's head. He paused. 'That is, of course, if you're interested in ships. Eh?' And he cocked his sharp little head to one side, quizzically.

'Oh, I am! I am!' squealed Mark hastily. 'I know ever such a lot about ships, Dad, really. You'll be surprised.'

'Look, David, isn't it marvellous?' he went on, turning to me.

'Jolly fine,' I said.

'And will it sail, Dad?' asked Mark. 'I mean, will it sail on the boating-lake?'

Uncle Walter looked ponderous. 'Why, to tell you the truth, lad, I hadn't thought about that ...'

He took a long, thoughtful look at the ship, picking it up and holding it away from him at arm's length, closing first one eye and then the other as if judging to a hair's breadth the miracle ship's possible qualifications for sailing on Penporth boating-lake.

'Well, anyway,' he said, 'she's a good ship, that's beyond doubt.'

He straightened up and stroked his chin, pretending to be taking grave deliberations, though all the time you could see the aroused light of excitement – the same as often came upon Mark – in his eyes.

'But I tell you what, boy,' he said suddenly. 'What say we go and try her out? See what we can manage, eh?'

'Oh, yes! Please, let's!' exclaimed Mark, and he half turned as if wanting to run off there and then.

'Oh – er – well –' Uncle Walter's confidence faded a little as he noticed Aunty Mags already sitting at the head of the tea-table, her hand resting impatiently on the tea cosy. 'Later, boy, later on.'

He jumped smartly to his feet.

'Now's the time for tea, eh? Good old cuppa tea, that's right.' And he put an arm extravagantly around Aunty Mags' shoulder and gave her a cupboard-love kiss on the cheek – before moving over to take his place next to Mark, ready to enliven and dominate the meal with his tales from all the world over.

Uncle Walter seemed very quickly at home. No doubt his confidence was helped by the evident reverence in which he was held, not only by his family but by the boarders. Mark among the children, and Aunty Mags, among the grown-ups, had spread an impression of a dynamic, almost mythical figure; a mixture of Captain Cuttle, Long John Silver, Francis Drake and Lord Nelson. Uncle Walter, it was true, was quite small in stature and his arrival in civilian garb had been rather unexpected. As against this, he was the owner of a striking pointed black beard, and the check suit, you might say, had a character all of its own.

When, on the second day, he condescended to wear his navy blue seaman's jersey and trousers, substituting a nautical, if battered, seaman's cap for his prim bowler hat, he firmly established himself as the favourite of the house. This position he strengthened very successfully by a flow of voluble and colourful conversation such as had probably not been heard at the house before. Every afternoon it was a common sight to find Uncle Walter established in the one comfortable deck-chair in the front garden, surrounded by an admiring group of children to whom he recounted lurid but tactfully chosen tales of life on the high seas. His soft, high-pitched voice rose and fell in the hot afternoon sleepiness, and his neat goatee beard rose and fell in harmony. Gradually, the voice faded, the beard stilled, and with quiet dignity Uncle Walter's head dropped forward, his bright little eyes shutting into sleep, and, regretfully, the children stole away to other pastimes.

In the mornings Uncle Walter led a sheltered life, remaining in bed (Aunty Mags always took up his breakfast after she had served and cleared away the guests' meals) until just before mid-day. About this time we might glimpse him hurrying down the stairs, dressed for going out. His greeting would be disappointingly abrupt and he would stride quickly out of the house and along the promenade towards the village. He would be certain, however, to return by one o'clock, for that was lunchtime, and then he would seem much more the real, lively Uncle Walter, a look of pink satisfaction possessing the face that had earlier seemed somewhat pinched and worried. It would be the same in the evening, and again when Uncle Walter returned it was in a mood of exhilaration sufficient to dominate the dinner-table conversation.

After a while we gathered, what with Uncle Walter's frequent smacking of lips and the suggestive aroma he breathed upon all and sundry, that his visits were to a certain family hotel up in the village, where the beer was of a brand that met with his not easily won approval. So, for us, the Rose and Crown, previously imagined as a sinister place full of evil, was transformed into an exciting fairy cavern designed principally to provide an adequate background for Uncle Walter – whom we saw, in our mind's eyes, the centre of a host of admiring listeners, quaffing mugs of foaming golden ale and recounting wonderful stories such as the one about how he sailed around the Cape in a three-master.

Although Uncle Walter protested several times that he had finished with the sea and was no longer a sailor at all, really, he was hardly given much opportunity to forget his nautical background – even if he had been able to do so. We knew that Uncle Walter had, at least in his last position, been a third mate on a cargo boat laden with iced meat, but he was seldom referred to by the villagers as anything much less than a Captain or a Commander. Once we heard Mr Brown of the Rose and Crown, call across to Uncle Walter, 'How are you, today, Rear-Admiral?' but then Mr Brown was rather one for his little joke.

Mind you, we were all of us glad enough to bask in the glamour that surrounded Uncle Walter. Aunty Mags, too, enjoyed her share of the limelight, and it was a pleasant sight to see her all dressed up for the Sunday service, walking along arm in arm with her very own husband – and him impressive in his best navy blue uniform, the buttons all shiny from Aunty Mags' diligent polishing of the previous evening. I rather wonder now if Uncle Walter understood, or cared much about what went on in the chapel. During the trembly falsetto preaching of Mr Hopkins, the minister, Uncle Walter's gaze would sometimes wander about aimlessly. However, if his eye happened to come to rest again upon Aunty Mags' shining, upturned face he would frown, as though with disgust at his own dilatoriness, and he, too, would look worshippingly upwards. He was terribly anxious to please Aunty Mags, always, was Uncle Walter, like the way he took her off to Penzance every Saturday afternoon, buying her a good fish and chip tea and then taking her in the best seats at one of the cinemas. He even made efforts to be useful about the house, and they must have been very real efforts, too, in the face of the temptation to take it easy in the deckchair, or have a sleep on the shingle across the way.

For a time Uncle Walter struggled nobly to do odd-jobs about the house, carrying visitors' luggage and giving a hand with washing up and so on. But it obviously made him more and more unhappy, and on hot days he used to perspire dreadfully, so we were all relieved when one day Uncle Walter confessed, a little shamefacedly, that perhaps he had better take things easy for fear of bringing on one of his attacks of fever.

'Yellow all over, I goes,' he said, sorrowfully. 'Yellow as a field of dandelions.'

'Indeed you must be careful, Walter. Take things nice and easy,' said Aunty Mags, fussily, and from then on, of course, she wouldn't hear of Uncle Walter lifting a finger.

With Uncle Walter to look after as well, I suppose Aunty Mags had quite a lot of extra work. She was always darning his socks and mending his shirts, and often she went into Penzance and bought something new for him. But she never grumbled, and indeed she probably had all the reward she wanted when she went walking along the prom on Uncle Walter's politely curved arm, nodding and smiling graciously to neighbours. For a brief-period, like a holiday you might say, the light of a young girl's happiness was winking in my Aunty Mags' eyes. It was only later, when Uncle Walter seemed to be out much more, and sometimes away all day wandering about – only then that you might come upon Aunty Mags looking quite a sad one, again. Once or twice I heard her heave a tiny sigh, on whose behalf I could never quite be sure. Perhaps because there were no nice, regular long letters to look forward to? I wondered. And perhaps, in a way, it was something like that.

Uncle Walter took a quick liking to Mark, and I, being Mark's friend, was accepted, too, though I was aware always of some extra intangible thread binding Mark and his father. It had something to do, I fancied, with the way Mark was always asking questions about the sea, and what was this ship like, and that ship, what was the longest voyage Uncle Walter had made and were there still any pirates at sea? In front of Aunty Mags you never caught Uncle Walter so much as breathe a word about the sea, and he would positively frown should Mark bring up the subject. But it was a very different story when we were away from the house – oh, a very different story, with Mark's questions quite swamped as Uncle Walter began remembering.

Many afternoons we used to go down to the boating-lake, Mark carrying the yacht proudly under one arm. We had christened her as *Walter II*, and Uncle Walter had painted the name along the bow, in red lettering. We used to set the sails and push her off from one corner, then run along the stone parapet, shouting over encouragements and warnings.

'She's listing to starboard,' Mark would shout out importantly.

'No, she isn't! She's going straight!' I would retaliate, an opposite reaction being automatic in those days.

Uncle Walter would bend down and shade his eyes and look very wise, and at last pronounce, 'She's all right, a bit shaky to lee, but all right,' – and we would run on, watching anxiously until *Walter II* at last had reached the other side, when Uncle Walter bent down expertly and caught the silver shaped bow just in time to save it from cracking against the stone edge.

Of course, it was greatest fun when someone else came along with another yacht and challenged a race. Then was the occasion for councils of war, weighty decisions to tilt the sails half an inch this way and the rudder a little more to one side, and so on. Thanks to Uncle Walter's superior judgment I don't think we ever lost a race.

After an afternoon at the boating-lake Uncle Walter would become quite as excited as us and look equally disappointed if Betty appeared on the scene to call out that tea was ready. But a meal was a meal, and one of Aunty Mags' something never to be missed, so back we went. Though I noticed that Betty, as often as not, used to walk ahead of us or behind us, and if Uncle Walter gave her one of his bluff, breezy hails, her smile was forced and distinctly faint.

Sometimes, after tea, Mark would persuade Uncle Walter to walk out along the point and there we would stand, in the familiar positions, shading eyes against the sun for a sight of a distant ship. It seemed that the sniff of the sea, blowing in extra fresh across the open bay, had much the same effect on Uncle Walter as whatever liquids he consumed at the Rose and Crown, for he would at once become his most voluble self. Standing there and listening to him it was easy – perhaps with a half closing of the eyes – to imagine yourself transplanted to the shore of some distant country. It was easy to imagine being at some busy harbour where ships from all over the world were lying at anchorage, some of them getting up steam, others unloading their cargo – hooters sounding, cranes groaning, waves lapping against the ships' hulls, here and there a fussy motor boat chugging about – or perhaps, if it was somewhere like Colombo, the long open native boats racing out to meet the steamers laden with bunches of bananas and coconuts, hoping for a quick and profitable sale – everywhere the babel of conflicting tongues, everywhere the smell of the sea, the stink of the dead fish and overthrown garbage.

'Aye, it's a strange life, and it always gets you,' said Uncle Walter meditatively. His arm on Mark's shoulder gave a tiny, instinctive tug. Then he suddenly broke into some sailor's song.

'Come on! Come on!' urged Uncle Walter. 'Join in the chorus, lads ... Now! One-two-three-off we go!' And he had us both singing with him at the tops of our voices against the not unmusical background of the waves splintering upon the nearby rocks.

As the weeks slipped by, however, Uncle Walter's glamour faded into familiarity, and he became just another villager at Penporth – while, no doubt, the newness of Penporth lost its attraction for him, too. As this happened he grew noticeably restless. Another odd thing was that he began getting up quite early in the morning, going out at a time long before any of the hotels would be open.

One day Mark and I followed him, discreetly, and found him sitting on a jetty outside Mr Stevens' boat-house, talking to the old man. Hitherto, the two sea-faring men had exchanged very little conversation, though they had always nodded in a friendly and mutually respectful way. Now, we gathered, Uncle Walter had taken to visiting Mr Stevens every morning. At first it was just a chat and a chin-wag over old sea stories. Then, as Mr Stevens was often called upon to take out some holiday-makers for a trip in his big motor-boat, Uncle Walter began standing at the boat-house doorway, so that if anyone else came along inquiring he could entertain them until Mr Stevens returned. But with trade fairly brisk it was not long before there was a small queue waiting, and so one day Uncle Walter turned to Mr Stevens as if he had just had a brilliant idea, and said:

'Why not let me take a party out in your other boat?'

Well, of course, that seemed as good an idea to Mr Stevens as it did to Uncle Walter, and that same morning Uncle Walter began taking visitors out in the other rowing-boat. As soon as there was room, of course, he took Mark and I – and real exciting that was, for when we had gone before with Mr Stevens the old man talked hardly a word, just rowed steadily along. With Uncle Walter at the oars the exercise – though obviously an effort – never dried up the vocabulary. Once again he had us singing sea shanties, and once again it was not hard to pretend we were on board some rather more exciting craft, sliding through shark-infested waters. I rather fancy that was what Uncle Walter rather imagined, too. At any rate I had not seen him looking so pleased for a long time as after that morning's work, when we were walking back to the house.

Yet when, at lunch-time, Aunty Mags looked over and inquired mildly if he had had an enjoyable morning, Uncle Walter looked quite guilty, flushing and muttering:

'Oh, so-so, Mags, so-so – just pottering about.' And he shot a sharp look at Mark and I which successfully curbed our itching tongues.

But, of course, Aunty Mags knew all about Mr Stevens. When we were coming back another morning I happened to look up and there she was standing at the window of her room, looking not at all like the cheery Aunty Mags we usually knew; though she was all her usual seeming cheerfulness at lunch. And another time, as Uncle Walter was rowing us across the bay, I watched the figures leaning along the promenade parapet, and I could have sworn one of them was Aunty Mags. She must have followed us very slowly; so wistful she looked, I fancied, way across the water, and I felt sad for her.

For Mark, in his seventh heaven, the next ambition was – could we not go for a trip on the Isles of Scilly steamer?

'Aye, indeed we shall!' called out Uncle Walter. And the very next day it was arranged that we should go.

This was too big a trip to try and keep to ourselves, and anyway we tried our best to get Aunty Mags to come along. She looked flustered, and hummed and hawed, and at last she said, 'Oh, dearie, I don't think I will, really – you know the sea upsets me so, Walter. And besides I couldn't possibly leave the house.'

Betty couldn't resist saying, Yes, she would come, for it was a natural treat to anyone, but I saw her mooning about and looking thoughtful in the way girls sometimes do, all that evening. When it came to setting out in the morning she came as far as the bus stage and then she stopped, looking as if she would burst into tears, and turned and ran all the way back again.

But Uncle Walter and I and Mark went, and I must say it was a fine outing, indeed. We walked up to the front of the boat, leaning on the rails and watching the sea coming to meet us, then we went to the back and watched and forked white trails left by the propellers. Uncle Walter took us on a tour of inspection, right down in the engine room ... for it did not take him long to get chatting to the engineer, nor for them to discover that they had once served in the same cargo line, out East.

At St Mary's, before we started back, Uncle Walter and the engineer went and had a drink at the pub. They bought Mark and me lemonades and Mark insisted we should go back and drink them standing on the ship, for fear it would leave without us.

'This is the life you know', he said, his eyes shining, '*this* is the life!' And as if clutching at each escaping minute he gulped down his drink and went hurrying round the ship again; while I leant over the rail and stared across the green swirling waters – to the grey rising mainland beyond.

When we got back Aunty Mags had kept a nice hot dinner for us, roast pork and apple sauce and fresh cream with damsons. It was a nice end to a nice day.

'Enjoy yourselves, did you?' she murmured.

'Oh, Mam, it was wonderful!' said Mark.

'Good,' said Aunty Mags. But I saw her look away and

frown. I didn't know much about what she might be thinking. Perhaps she was trying to remind herself what a fine outing it would be for any boy. But all the time, I noticed, Betty was watching her mother, and a look of something intangible, but possibly traceable to pity, coloured the look. It was then, momentarily, I had a sudden understanding: Why, Betty is growing up, growing up – and, why, isn't she like Aunty Mags! Though the thought was quickly lost, at the time.

I could see nothing much to frown about that evening, but I suppose Aunty Mags was wiser for her years than a boy of fourteen who only saw fragments. For, the very next day, Uncle Walter after pottering about at Stevens's sent a message that he wouldn't be back to lunch. We did not see him again until about the same time as the previous evening.

'Just took a little jaunt in the steamer, I did,' he explained defensively.

'Good, do you good, dear,' murmured Aunty Mags.

But Mark, of course, was very sad at having missed the trip, and he demanded that he be taken another time.

'Well, Mark,' said Uncle Walter, and he looked a little slyly at Aunty Mags, 'see what your mother says, eh?'

'What?' said Aunty Mags flatly, as if she hadn't heard; though you knew she had.

'Very well,' she said, after a pause. 'Very well.'

So the next day Uncle Walter took Mark with him, while I decided to stay and go for a walk with Betty. And the day after Uncle Walter went again, Mark, too, and the day after that. Each time they returned brimming over the excitements of the day's adventure.

'Why don't you go with them?' said Betty as we walked along the point one afternoon.

'Oh, perhaps I will soon,' I said, awkwardly, for I could not really have explained the diffidence that held me back.

'Why don't you go?' I countered.

'Don't know,' said Betty abruptly. We walked on for a while in silence.

'Yes I do,' she said abruptly. 'Yes I do. It's because you can't trust ships. You're always at their mercy, and they're always at the sea's mercy and the sea's always at the weather's mercy – and so on and so on. And yet when you go on a ship you have to give yourself up altogether to the ship alone, never mind anything else ... It's silly, that's what I think. I like to have my two feet on the land and lead my own way,' said Betty, pouting a little, and then giving me a rather shy, sweetly innocent smile.

'Yes,' I said quickly, sensing a sudden harmony I had never known with Mark. 'That's how I feel about it, too.'

When I got back and was climbing the stairs I heard Uncle Walter talking to Aunty Mags, in their bedroom. Something about the tone of the voices made me stop and try to listen. One of the voices, Uncle Walter's, kept getting louder and then softer, and I realised that he must be walking up and down the room. It was Uncle Walter's voice talking nearly all the time, and whenever it paused all I heard Aunty Mags say was a single word, or perhaps two. Because of the closed door I could not distinguish much of what was said, save that Uncle Walter seemed to be trying to persuade Aunty Mags about something; rather as if he were justifying something, or trying to assure her about something. All the time I was still with nervousness lest someone should come up the stairs and catch me eavesdropping – or, worst of all, lest Uncle Walter's footsteps should bring him suddenly to the door.

Yet there was a certain meaning about the talking that forced itself through the door and into my consciousness. It was something about how Uncle Walter was racing on till he was breathless as though frightened that if he stopped he would fail to convince himself or his audience – and how Aunty Mags had no volubility at all, just as if her mind had resigned itself to something inevitable and there was no more to be said, and there was really no need for Uncle Walter to go on talking and pretending the impossible.

I don't know how the conversation ended, for one of the boarders came up the stairs and I had to scurry away into my room. But the very next morning Uncle Walter was up as early as anyone else, his face set into the stern lines of one who was determined to show that a fresh start could be made. To our astonishment he kept bustling about from kitchen to dining-room and back again, helping to serve up the breakfast, afterwards stacking up the trays and tackling the washing-up. He was very jovial and cheerful, humming away to himself, and above all, I noticed, extra pleasant towards Aunty Mags. Moreover he announced that today, for a change, there would be no trip on the steamer (though to alleviate Mark's evident disappointment he also agreed, quietly, to come along to the boating-pool in the afternoon). Several times he referred to this generous abstinence, in front of Aunty Mags, as though anxious to make sure that she appreciated the gesture. Aunty Mags nodded and smiled faintly as she methodically wiped the dishes after Uncle Walter had swished them round in the greasy water.

For some reason, just as Uncle Walter was appearing at his apparent jolliest, so Aunty Mags seemed to have sunk down into an unfamiliar gloom. Something of the colour and laughter was missing from her face. Suddenly I realised that Aunty Mags looked very tired, and quite a little old from the tiredness, as though she found life too great a problem.

Towards midday you could see the strain beginning to tell on Uncle Walter. At last he quietly took off his apron, folded it neatly, and then, after pacing awkwardly about the kitchen, disappeared upstairs. He re-appeared later, spruce and freshened, twirling an old walking stick in one hand, and went off to the village.

When Uncle Walter returned it was later than usual and we were already started at lunch, but he did not seem to mind at all. Indeed he made quite a dramatic entry, sweeping open the door and taking his hat off in a flourishing bow to the people in the room. After coming with a slow, swaggering gait over to our table, he insisted on pulling his chair round beside Aunty Mags and proceeded to eat a hearty lunch to the accompaniment of many extravagant gestures and remarks. It was evident that Uncle Walter's visit to the family hotel in the village had been devoted to some rather extra celebrations. He had brought back a very fat cigar which he was still smoking, in long, thick blasts of smoke. And somehow or other he had obtained a bright red carnation, now fixed prominently in his lapel.

'Do you think p'raps it's his birthday?' whispered Betty at the other end of the table, to me.

I had not before associated birthdays and Uncle Walter, but the idea became at once intriguing. In its wake started all sorts of other ideas, and I began to wonder for the first time how old Uncle Walter was, and where he was born and who were his mother and father and how he came to meet Aunty Mags and why and how and why. It struck me suddenly that, of course, Uncle Walter was not Cornish but Aunty Mags was; and, how funny, Uncle Walter might have come from a long long way away, but Aunty Mags was born and bred in Penporth. And my mind was thrown into confusion at the alternate wonders how small was the world and how large was the world.

But Uncle Walter, birthday or not, had obviously enjoyed his outing, and he continued to beam on all and sundry. He seemed, behind his jovial facade, to be possessed, supremely, with a desperate desire to give pleasure to Aunty Mags: as though in some obscure way the sands of time were running short. When packets of jolly conversation failed Uncle Walter, in his current mood of exuberance, raised a benevolent, husbandly hand and patted it upon Aunty Mags ample back, then slipped it under Aunty Mags' plump elbow and gave a friendly squeeze. Aunty Mags smiled faintly, looking sideways at Uncle Walter with a look that was neither disapproving or approving, but more like a look of pity.

After a time she gently moved away, disentangling her arm. As the mild rebuff penetrated to Uncle Walter's consciousness he shook his head sorrowfully and, for a moment, fell into morose contemplation of the twisting reflections of a glass of water. At last pulling himself together with a start, he gave a broad, false grin and began all over again with his jolly jokes and his gestures of love and kindliness. It was then, remembering sitting in a cinema and watching the programme round twice, I realised that Uncle Walter was acting.

When, later in the afternoon, Uncle Walter came along to

the boating-pool Mark greeted him excitedly, clinging to his arm with a rush of affection that, I fancy, brought moisture to his father's eyes. It was difficult to be sure because Uncle Walter's eyes had suddenly become rather small and bloodshot, and he was blinking a lot. Whether it was the morning's revelry or just tiredness I would not like to say but he did not seem to see as clearly as usual, and altogether he seemed to be immersed in some morose inner conflict. None of this was noticed by Mark, however, as he pulled Uncle Walter towards the pool; nor would I have noticed it if I had been Mark I am sure.

It was one of those afternoons we sometimes used to experience at Penporth when a bad-tempered wind came lashing the sea into a white froth, flicking about viciously so that the landscape, as well, took on a ruffled appearance. The sun was high and bright as usual but the light had a false tint, so that altogether it would have been difficult for anyone to feel like sitting about and dozing. At the boating-pool the water, usually placid, was chopped into grey-white waves that broke angrily against the banks – just like the real sea would be breaking against the rocks out on the headland.

'This'll give *Walter II* a chance to show her paces, won't it, Dad?' exclaimed Mark. He stood with his feet astride and the yacht sheltered under him. The wind that blew Mark's unruly hair all over the place also rustled and tugged irritably among the intricate sails of *Walter II*.

'Eh?' said Uncle Walter. 'Yes,' he said a moment later, as if his mind needed more time than usual to grapple with questions. 'It's a good hard blow.'

He turned for a moment and stared out across the sands, shading his eyes.

'Choppy out there. I wonder – I wonder –' And then he fell silent.

'I bet you've seen choppier seas than this, Dad,' declared Mark proudly.

'Eh? ... Oh, I have that, yes.' Uncle Walter gave one of his old breezy laughs, and clapped a hand on Mark's shoulder. 'Why, Mark my boy, I've seen seas that come towards you like a wall, higher than your own head, straight for you and then smashing down over the whole ship ... And not once, mind you, not once or twice, or three times, but again and again and again. Yes, and I remember once in the Pacific. We were doing a trip to Tahiti, in the fishing season. We were five days at sea, and an afternoon rather like this ... bright sun, angry sea, sort of day you could sense trouble in the air. Well, it was towards evening and –'

Uncle Walter pressed his lips tight together, then curled the lower one outwards, thoughtfully.

'Yes,' he said musingly. 'Well ... come on, now. What about the yacht, boy, what about the yacht?'

And, since Mark was temporarily more interested in the yacht than his father's stories, he led the way down to the water and we gathered round for the preliminary excitement of preparing *Walter II* to take the sea.

But, as Uncle Walter had been saying, it was one of those trouble days. I think, now perhaps it was in the air and he, too, sensed it. Once or twice I saw him hesitate and stand up, looking about pensively; though I must say I thought he was looking much further away than the boating-pool. At any rate it took more time than usual to get the yacht ready and when, at last, it was time to put her into the water Uncle Walter fumbled, not with his usual sure touch but in a clumsy, rather hopeless fashion – as though his bloodshot eyes could not cope with such a serious intricate affair as *Walter II*, because they were searching elsewhere.

Perhaps Mark did not notice any of this, for as soon as the yacht was in the water he cried out his usual jubilant 'O.K – let her go! Let her go!'

At the familiar call Uncle Walter automatically gave *Walter II* a shove, and a moment later the long, graceful bow was cutting out into the tossing, choppy waves. There were no other yachts about at that time, though quite a few people were watching. The three of us stood there watching the yacht slashing its path forward, leaving the faint trail of white. Soon the wind was blowing really hard, angrily and with increasing force, until one or two of the outer sails began to balloon outwards. The next moment the yacht heeled drunkenly: then, as she straightened, turned to the left. Suddenly it seemed that she was streaking forward at phenomenal speed, out of our control.

Mark shouted out, urgently:

'Oh! Look! Look out, she's going into the bank!' He began running down the side.

A moment later Uncle Walter gave a sharp cry of alarm to show his realisation of the danger. But by the time he had run along the bank it was too late: and Mark was too late as well.

We saw *Walter II* ride across the waves with a proud, almost disdainful elegance. But she was riding out of track... she came in at full speed and cracked head-on against the hard, cement stone bank of the boating-lake. The crack sent a shudder right through her, tossed her to one side, then one of the angry waves caught her sideways and cracked her against the bank. This time the yacht caught a tiny over-flow pipe that jutted out a few inches from the bank. The impact smashed into the delicate woodwork and with a wail and a gurgle the water swallowed *Walter II*.

Uncle Walter fished out the yacht with the curved end of his walking stick; but it was not the yacht of a moment ago, all sleek and shining. It looked cold and bedraggled, the sails limp and soggy and a sudden atmosphere of desolation about the decks; the forecastle bent in and one of the masts leaning over drunkenly. He held the yacht in his two tattooed hands, turning it slowly over and over, staring at it with a most peculiar, hypnotised expression on his face – mumbling to himself, every now and then, 'Out of place, out of place in a boating-lake – don't you see, it was bound to happen – don't you see, she was out of place...?' And then staring sadly at the yacht that would never again be the same, while Mark stood dry-eyed and tense, watching and watching.

The next morning Uncle Walter put on his best sailor's suit, slung his kit-bag over his shoulder, and walked out of the house. He never looked back as he went away down the promenade, for Betty and I watched him from the sitting-room window. And he never came back.

Ah, it was a long time ago but I remember it like yesterday – the whole, long, dreamlike day, with life outwardly going on the same as ever, with Aunty Mags herself acting unconcerned the whole day long, just so that Mark's discovery of what had happened should be delayed a while. Poor Mark! I can see him now wandering about, worriedly, eventually coming and saying:

'It's funny, I can't find dad anywhere, not even at Mr Stevens.' And Betty and I looking in each other's eyes and knowing, just like Aunty Mags knew. And how sad it was at the end of the day, with the pretending over and Mark crying for the first time I could remember, crying like he would spill the heart out of him with the tears – yet all of a sudden drying up into an unnatural, ominous silence.

That evening, Aunty Mags picked up her sewing basket and took out some socks and coloured mending cottons and began sewing, her face bent downwards into its own shadows. The big sideboard clock ticked and tocked and ticked and tocked, the long gable windows rattled at the idle flicks of an evening wind; outside the light turned yellow and then rust-brown and then a silver grey, and we knew the sun was setting as usual, just the end of another day. But none of us ventured to look out, or break the quiet pattern of the fireside circle – none of us except Mark, that is, for he seemed to find it impossible to sit still and was forever moving about the room, fingering things and looking restless and unhappy, as well he might. And all the time that Mark moved about Aunty Mags kept flicking up her eyes from their sewing, to see what he was doing. Whenever I looked sideways at her I saw a frown formed across her forehead, and though it faded when she looked down at her sewing, everytime she watched Mark it grew fresh and strong again, and began to look like it was there forever.

And when Mark turned from looking out of the window and said, sharply, 'Shall we go out along the headland, David?' – why Aunty Mags, of all people, seemed to jump out of her chair, and her voice jumped out as well, crying with unfamiliar harshness:

'No! No, indeed, not along the headland ... It's too late ...

It's too late ... It's ... It's ...'

Then, as quick as it came, the harshness broke, the voice sagged and faded away. Aunty Mags gave a long sigh, and sank back into her chair, waving her hand in a gesture of helpless resignation. With a glance at me Mark led the way out of the room, into the cool night air, and we set off towards the headland.

I expect when we had gone Aunty Mags shed a tear or two and touched a fond hand through Betty's placid golden hair, for comfort. Perhaps she felt a little happier then. Because I have no doubt at all but that Aunty Mags had no need to come with us to know the sort of look that was on Mark's face as we stood on the tip of the headland that night, staring out over the dark restless sea. It was a look Aunty Mags must have seen several times in her long life, whereas I had never seen its like before.

It was the look on Uncle Walter's face that afternoon when he stood beside the choppy waters of the boating-lake and decided to walk out of Aunty Mags' life and return to the sea. The very same look.

II

The Face in the Mirror

I saw him watching me in the wide mirror of the barber's saloon. He was a wiry, little man of about forty, with a round bullet-like head, going bald. He was drably dressed in baggy flannels and a faded brown jacket, with a mackintosh over one arm and slouching trilby hat balanced on his knees. He seemed a subdued and insignificant figure, yet there was something disturbingly familiar about him. His face, which was rather ugly, with protruding front teeth and deep, unsightly eye-sockets, was not a stranger's face. Something about it provoked in me an odd feeling of impending surprise, of startled recognition to come. I felt I ought to have known his face immediately, but somehow it remained shadowy and indefinable – slightly, and worryingly, outside the focus of my understanding.

It was about four o'clock and I had dropped in for a shave on my way home from work. I was leaning back with my eyes half-closed, pretending to be immersed in an animated conversation with the barber, and I don't think the little man realized I had observed his interest. I remembered that he had come into the barber's shop just behind me. I had taken the proffered shaving chair, while he had taken off his hat and mackintosh and sat down on the bench for waiting customers. As far as I knew, he had picked up one of the newspapers on the bench and started reading it. It was only by chance, while the barber was filling the hot-water mug from a can in the corner, that I happened to look in the mirror and see the little man staring across the room with bright, burning eyes. With sudden uneasiness I realized his gaze was aimed specifically in my direction. It was not a casual, not a mildly curious gaze, but rather the fierce, almost wolfish gaze of a man who had suddenly set eyes on a prey for which he had long been seeking. The eyes seemed to burn into the mirror with a sort of consuming hatred. I felt a chill creep into my reclining body. Of course, I was being quite ridiculous, I told myself, fighting hard against a tremendous desire to turn my head away and pretend it was all a dream. I was imagining things. In a moment or so I would see the man's eyes drift away and return in bored unconcern to their newspaper. But, unfortunately, they did not. They remained, instead, fixed unwaveringly upon me, two pin-points of steely menace that bored into my very existence. They seemed to be alight with an evil flame, and they were growing brighter and brighter.

I stuck it for a while, wriggling uncomfortably in my seat and trying unsuccessfully to let the monotone of the barber's voice lull me into a sense of security. Then I felt the little man's gaze becoming fiercer, more impelling, and I began to get really perturbed.

'For God's sake, hurry up and finish!' I muttered to the barber out of the corner of my mouth, so that the little man wouldn't notice. I drummed my fingers nervously on the side of the chair while the barber, disgruntled, gave a hasty wipe of a towel over my face, then roughly whisked off the cover sheet.

As I rose from the chair I looked casually into the mirror. The eyes of the little man rose upwards with me, following my movements steadily. I couldn't be quite sure (his face was still blurred), but it seemed that a quick look of cunning flitted across his face, as if he were making some rapid decision to cope with the new problem created by my imminent departure. For a moment I hesitated, wondering if he would rise and dutifully take the seat which the barber was now politely offering to him. Indeed, he was beginning to rise – but some flash of intuition warned me that he had no intention of taking the seat. I hastily thrust a coin into the barber's hand. 'Keep the change!' I said hurriedly. Then I grabbed up my mackintosh and hat and ran out of the shop, swinging the door back behind me viciously.

I didn't dare to look back, but I felt sure that the little man had come after me. I began walking down the street as fast as I could without actually running, intent on finding some sort of hiding place. When I came to a Woolworth's on the corner, I darted through the entrance. Inside, there was a thick crowd of shoppers: I threaded my way among them, burrowing deeper and deeper into the mass of sticky humanity. When I reached the stationery counter at the far end of the shop, I felt safer. Looking back I could see a jumble of housewives, old men and children, but no sign of the little man. I breathed easier and began walking slowly up and down the counter. I felt a tempting sensation of relief stealing over me. It would be all right now. Probably the little man's view had been temporarily blocked at the particular moment I stepped into Woolworth's. He would have gone hurrying by ... I would give him a few minutes, then come out of the shop and get a bus home.

I began wandering from counter to counter, looking at the goods with idle curiosity. I passed from stationery to kitchenware, then to hardware, then back to stationery. Passing the hardware counter for the third time, I felt the assistant eyeing me, and hastily picked up a coloured mixing bowl. 'I'll take this,' I said, smiling brightly at her. She took my silver and moved away to get change.

I found myself smiling into a long rather dirty mirror which lined the wall behind the counter. I went on smiling rather mechanically, then felt the grin slowly freeze across my face. Standing at the counter behind me I could see the little man, his slouch hat pulled down over his eyes, his mackintosh thrown untidily over his shoulder. He was pretending to examine a writing pad, but all the time his eyes were darting round the shop. Feeling like a hypnotized rabbit, I stood there without moving and watched his gaze travel round until it alighted, abruptly, on me. For a moment we remained like two statues; then the little man started to move. I had an extraordinary feeling that he was going to vault over the counter towards me.

Crying out in sudden terror, I dropped the bowl on to the

edge of the counter, cracking it into a dozen pieces, and started running down the corridor leading to the nearest exit. Behind me I heard the startled cry of the assistant; shoppers and other assistants turned a sea of surprised faces in my direction; but before they could make any move to stop me, I had plunged through an exit swing-door. As I did so I fancied I caught a glimpse of the little man irritably pushing his way through a converging crowd of people.

Outside in the street again I felt bare and defenceless, like an animal caught in the open. Seeing another big store on the other side of the road, I made a dash for it, skipping neatly across the path of a tram and passing smoothly through a revolving door. As I went in I looked across the road and saw the Woolworth's door bursting open, and I knew that he was after me.

This was one of the higher-class stores, mostly clothing and drapery. The tall counters and drooping fabrics offered some excellent cover. I hurriedly skirted round the shop, keeping an occasional eye on the entrance to see if the little man would come in. Unfortunately, while doing this I backed into a precarious tower of carpet rolls and brought the whole lot tumbling down, spread-eagling me on to the floor. Terrified by a sudden fear that the little man would come leaping down on me, I scrambled to my feet and started running away without waiting to repair the damage – taking with me a blurred vision of a shop-walker's stout, reddening face, convulsed with indignation. I went on, turning two or three corners, passing through the ladies' underwear and brassiere sections. Then I began to wonder whether, during my accident, the little man had entered the shop and was even now waiting for me behind some tall display stand. It would certainly be safer to transfer myself to some other floor. Looking around I saw a convenient sign pointing: LIFTS. I hurried along and, in luck's way, I found the lift waiting, the uniformed girl about to close the gates.

'Hey, wait!' I cried, running up. The girl smiled demurely and stepped aside. I went in and flopped on to a welcome bench. The girl called out: 'Going up!' Some other passengers crowded in after me. Then she clanged the gate and the lift started rising.

Something made me take uneasy stock of my surroundings. My nearest neighbours were two faded old ladies, out for an afternoon's shopping. Next to them were a mother and her small girl. Beyond her ... beyond her I caught a glimpse of the side of a man's face. There was something about it. One of the old ladies turned, sweeping her wide-brimmed hat out of my line of vision. Then indeed, I nearly died. The little man was standing exactly opposite with only one or two women between us.

At the sight of me a ferocious grin split his face into an evil mask. His drawn-back lips seemed about to mouth fearful epithets. For the first time I realized how incomparably sinister a figure he was, how threatening was the whole of his hard, shrivelled-up menacing presence. Now, indeed, there was no longer any room for doubt, no chance of pretending otherwise than that it was a chase for life or death.

My tongue parched in my mouth. I tried to utter words.

'Help!' I said. 'Help!'

I thought I was crying out, but the words must have stuck in my throat.

'What floor did you say?' said the lift-girl, looking at me.

I didn't reply. I just stared fascinatedly at the little man, and he stared back at me. I noticed he had a small unkempt moustache and a stubble of beard, and a sharp pointed nose. (I suddenly thought of a miniature Mephistopheles.) At any moment he would brush aside the old ladies with a wave of his hand.

'Third floor,' said the lift-girl unemotionally.

'Here, let me get out!' I cried wildly. With a terrific surge of strength I seized one of the old ladies around her waist and half-lifted, half-threw her into the path of the little man. Then I dived out of the lift, knocking the surprised lift-girl against the side. Seeing some stairs running beside the lift-shaft, I darted to them and began bounding down them two at a time. I heard someone call out after me: 'He must be mad! Stop him!' It was probably the old lady. Or, more likely, the little fellow. He would be after me down the stairs, like a terrier.

I beat him to the exit, however. I flew out of that store even faster than I had left Woolworth's. This time I gave up all pretence and began running hell-for-leather down the street. I saw people staring at me, and a policeman raised his eyebrows, but I didn't care how much attention I aroused. I only wanted to get a long way away. I ran the whole length of the main shopping street and then took a turning at random into a smaller, secondary street. I was puffing: it was some years since I had done any running. The trouble was my lunch was still a weight on me. It had been a good and heavy one ... And I bitterly regretted my two mild and bitters. I could hear them swishing about inside me.

Looking back I couldn't see any sign of the little man; so I slackened my run to a panting walk. I wasn't fool enough to think I had given him the slip, but at least I had time to think and manoeuvre. Although I could hear my heart beating with heavy thuds, I felt much cooler in the head. I remembered reading in detective stories that danger sharpened the brain. Well, something like that was happening to me. It was high time I forgot all about how, three-quarters of an hour ago, I had been walking home from work, like I had done for nineteen years, and how I'd thought it might be a good idea to have a shave. (I like now and then to have the thing done professionally.) It was high time I forgot all about that and concentrated on the job in hand. Here I was, walking down a dusty side street which I didn't rightly recognize, going in the opposite direction to my home in the suburbs ... and not far behind a little man with a bullet head was after me, peeping in and out of the shop fronts. (I gave him credit for that: he looked a thorough sort.) I would have to fox him, and fox him properly. It couldn't be done lightly: it had to be thought out carefully.

I seemed to be moving into the business quarters. I passed big blocks of offices, inhabited by hundreds of formal, unknown 'Messrs.' I wondered whether to slip into one of the buildings and hide for a while, but decided the risk of arousing suspicion, possibly of being captured by a truculent commissionaire, was too great. I went on, walking about twice as fast as would ordinarily be the case. It was tiring, but it helped to keep up my morale. I kept crossing from one side of the road to another, and taking right turnings and then left turnings. In this way I reckoned to mix the little man up a good deal. Also, in the process, I got myself completely lost. Indeed, I was gradually overcome by a fantastic feeling that I was now in a completely strange town, without any knowledge of locality or direction. It was possible that, in fact, many of the streets were normally familiar to me. But as I turned down one street and up another, I began to feel that I was in some gigantic maze, whose towering walls were nebulous and unreal. Twice I became so lost that I found myself back at a street corner which I had passed a few moments previously. On the third occasion that this happened I found myself walking back on my tracks and saw, some way ahead of me, a disturbance at a street-crossing. I didn't know how he had done it but I guessed that the little fellow was on my trail again, pushing his way through a crowd. I turned round and began running again.

It was exciting in a way. There was always the persistent thrill of danger, arising out of the knowledge that I was being chased. There was, too, always the possibility of my coming round a corner and walking straight into the little man. I wondered which of us would have the presence of mind to act first. I rather prided myself that we would at least be about even. I had worked out a very neat plan for lowering my head, butting him hard in the stomach and then dashing away – when coming round a corner I bumped straight into a tall, heavy policeman, knocking him sideways and staggering backwards myself.

'I'm terribly sorry, officer,' I said.

Then I didn't wait for any more because I recognized his face and knew that I had already walked past him four times, in four different streets. I had a dim idea that he shouted something after me, but by that time I had disappeared down an alleyway. It was a very long alley, and towering buildings shut out most of the light. I walked along it feeling more and more alone and frightened. When I eventually emerged from it into a rather dingy shopping street, I was so exhausted – after three imaginary encounters in the shadows with the little man, and one terrifying episode in which I saw the policeman starting towards me out of a lamp-post – that there was sweat dripping off my forehead and a weak feeling in my legs.

That's the trouble with being chased. It doesn't matter really who's chasing you: if it goes on long enough, it gets to the stage where you feel like everyone's chasing you. For instance, it wasn't long before I was going round not only with the little man and the big policeman on my track, but also with the knowledge that if I passed their way again at least three other people (a vegetable stall man, a newspaper seller and a squat Jewish woman shopkeeper) would decide I was either a criminal or a madman, and start chasing me themselves. For that reason I made a concentrated effort to move steadily away from the district where I had been wandering for an hour or so. When I came out into the shopping street, one of the suburban type, I knew that I was succeeding to some extent. The street was less crowded – there was more space between the buildings – and the trams had that emptying look, as if they were penetrating further and further out of the town.

All this time, it was true, I hadn't seen the little man. But I knew that he was after me. There was something so very sure about him that I felt he wouldn't be thrown off easily. Indeed, I remembered once seeing a film about something like that, where a fellow was chased all over the place by a gunman. No matter what this man did, the gunman kept tracking him down. In the end he cornered him in his own sitting-room, with his wife in a faint on the floor, and shot him three times through the head. It turned out, of course, that the fellow being chased had played a dirty trick on the gunman in the past; so it was all made to seem quite reasonable. My trouble was that I felt quite sure that the little man would keep finding me, but I couldn't for the life of me think of any reason for his interest. It was possible he hadn't got a gun (I shivered – his eyes were bad enough). But it was possible he had. I was glad that I hadn't gone home, following my first impulse; at least I wouldn't drag my wife into it. I hadn't forgotten my wife. I knew that already she would be somewhat worried. Most evenings I got home by five o'clock and we always had supper at six; now it was well after six, and getting to be dusk. Several times I thought, 'Well, I'll phone her, anyway,' and crossed over to a telephone box. But each time I went inside and heard the door bang on me, a terrifying feeling came over me. There I was, all nicely cooped up in an oblong box. The next moment I would see the little man glaring in through the glass panes. The moment I had that thought I pushed back the door and dashed out of the box. What's more, I was always pretty sure that if I hadn't done so, he would have been round the corner and on top of me.

I felt happier on the move. The trouble was that I had suddenly become conscious of my physical body. It was tired, dead tired. Not for ten years had I walked and run so much. My head urged me to wander on until I had shaken off the little man. My legs and the rest of my body just ached and ached. Aching like that can wear down anything, even the most rigid of purposes. It just goes on and on, gets heavier and wearier, until you feel you'll drop down dead about three steps forward. I didn't see much point in that. I began looking around for some shelter. Besides, it was getting dark, and there might be some real chance of giving him the slip.

I picked in the end on a small cinema, tucked away among a block of shops. It suddenly struck me as a brilliant idea. I fished two bob out of my pocket and darted in, thrusting the money at the box-office girl, grabbing the ticket and plunging into the welcome darkness. It was all smoky and hazy inside, but it was shelter. I found a seat at the end of a row. It was soft and cushioned ... I sank into it with a sensuous feeling of pleasure on the arm rests. I turned my attention to the screen and tried to forget about the little man.

It was about two minutes from the end of the big picture – something about a matador in Spain, the scene a bullfight finale – when I heard the little man coming into the cinema. There's no way of explaining how or why: I just knew it was him. There was a faint light from the door; then I saw a shadow – a small shadow – floating down the aisle. There wasn't any girl or anyone else, just him. He was pretending to be a stranger, looking round casually for a seat. But I was watching him like a hawk and I saw him stop at the end of my row and slide himself into the first seat. A moment later he was sitting in the fifth seat; then he'd dropped into the seventh seat. There were four seats between him and me, and the bull in the film was just making its death charge, when I leaped out of my seat and fled towards the cinema exit. It was a familiar feeling; only this time I did it quicker than ever before. I fancy even the little man was surprised.

It was dark when I got outside. It gave me a feeling of security, just like the cinema. I began loitering past the shops, trying to catch the sound of the little man's footsteps. The next thing that happened was someone shone a torch full on me, dazzling me, bathing me in relentless light. There wasn't time for any thinking. I just lowered my head and made a wild rush at the light. I think my head went about straight into the centre of a stomach. The light went out and I heard a strangled 'Ouch!' of pain. I must admit it gave me a thrill of sadistic pleasure, that moment. The action was so completely and devastatingly successful. It put me temporarily in supreme control of the situation. I felt a shadow sprawling on the pavement and started running away into the darkness. The wind was on my face as I vanished into the darkness ... Indeed, it was almost exhilarating.

I guessed that had made him mad. I heard some shouting and saw the torch come on again, whirling savagely. I also heard the surprising sound of a shrill whistle. A few minutes later there was an answering whistle somewhere ahead of me. These things, happening one after the other, got me rather confused, but I had enough presence of mind to take a turning and sprint down it deep into the night.

I had to stop running pretty soon. I had to lean against a lamp-post and take great heaving breaths. Otherwise I felt I should have collapsed. I stood there for several tense moments getting my breath back and at the same time listening for the sound of chasing footsteps. But by some miracle the quiet remained unbroken. My ears had to be content with the dull rustle of wind in the tree-tops that lined the road and with far-off occasional hoots of cars. It was very eerie – very eerie indeed.

For, I suddenly realized, because there were no footsteps it did not mean I was not being followed. I would be a fool not to concede more than average intelligence to the little man. He was the sort, I decided, visualizing his small, crafty face, alive with hidden cunning, who would possibly wrap cloth over his boots – or even take them off. In a flash all sense of temporary relief vanished. Standing there I became aware, with a blinding horror, that every shadow, however vague, every rustle, however muffled, might not be what it seemed. Even the solid shapes of the trees might not be real ... I think it was when I got to that state of mind that I gave up all efforts to preserve my morality, my sense of ethics, my character of an ordinary citizen who some hours previously had been sitting in his respectable office, doing his respectable job. There, swimming in the menacing shadows of a suburban residential street, I gave it all up and became the hunted fugitive, the animal who must use his cunning – not only to outwit his chaser, but to dispose of him.

I can remember how clear and simple it all became. It was as if a tremendous load had fallen away. I felt a wave of confidence pouring into me. At the same time I felt myself in powerful control of my senses, became aware of newly-acquired strength. I waited not in fear, but in expectancy, for what I knew would eventually come. I didn't mind how long the wait now that I knew exactly what course of action to follow, exactly what events were going to take place. And it was a long wait. I felt the cold night air creeping into my clothes, enveloping my feet, my fingers, my ears, sinking into my limbs. I didn't dare stamp or flap my arms for fear of giving my position away. For now, the whole essence of success was surprise. I had moved close into the shadow of a tree, merging myself into its frame. I could not possibly be seen against that dark outline. There I waited, breathing as quietly as possible, hardly daring to move a muscle. In fact, I felt it would be dangerous even to think – I might weaken in my new resolve – so I deliberately devoted my mind to counting numbers.

I had reached one hundred and forty-five, I think, when I heard him coming. Probably to anyone else it would have sounded just like a rustle of wind in the trees, or a leaf blowing about – but, of course, that was just what he would have wanted me to think. I envisaged now his triumphant smile, his sense of achievement, and smiled to myself. There was hardly any sound, just that faint, occasional, apparently casual rustle. I can't imitate the sound in writing, but it was rather like somebody turning over the pages of a newspaper. And that, of course, reminded me of how I had first seen him, sitting there in the barber's shop, so insignificant, so innocent. A huge burning indignation swept over me at the thought of all the trouble he had given me. What had I ever done to him? Who was he to hound me down like a criminal? What right had he to bring terror into my life? It would take me weeks to recover from that one evening. And my wife – God knows what she would be thinking.

I had just reached the apex of these thoughts when I saw him. He was only a few feet away from me – the vaguest of shadows – but a sixth sense told me that it was him. He was sliding along, like some dirty, little sneak thief. I counted as he came nearer, giving him a certain number of steps to come level. One – two – three – four – five – six. 'Seven,' I said out loud, or I might even have shouted it, to startle him. Then I leapt forward and clutched him, and we went rolling on the ground.

I had taken him completely by surprise. I was able to get my hands round his neck just where I wanted to. I knew exactly what to do: I had read it all in considerable detail in a crime novel. I held my fingers firmly into the flesh of his neck, pressing my body hard down on him, and with my two thumbs I felt for the narrow stem of his windpipe. I had got him – I knew I had got him. I could feel him suddenly struggling convulsively, like a drowning man. I maintained my grip, pressing tighter and tighter. I could feel my nails cutting into the flesh of his neck. I could hear the breath ebbing out of him. My stranglehold sank deeper and deeper ... Then, suddenly, like an immense nightmare, the darkness seemed to swoop down on me, pouring over me in a gigantic wave of pain. Conscious of a helpless, detached sensation of bewilderment, I felt myself falling away ... falling, falling, falling ... down into a deep, black oblivion.

When I opened my eyes again it was no longer dark, but bright daylight. I was no longer fighting for my life in a quiet back street, but lying in bed in a hospital ward, with sunshine pouring through a window and falling in great streaks across the white coverlet.

There was a white-coated nurse sitting at a table in one corner. When she saw me open my eyes, she got up and came over. She was smiling – somehow it warmed me through and through to see her smile. I felt I just wanted to lie back there and drowse away, with everything big and white and peaceful, with the sunshine pouring in, and the nurse smiling. But there was something stopping me, something small and hard-pressing far away at the back of my mind. I didn't quite know what it was, and I couldn't quite express myself.

I looked up beseechingly at the nurse. She smiled and bent down, putting a cool hand on my head.

'It's all right, you just relax,' she said. 'You've had a nasty experience, a terrible shock, but you're going to be all right now. You just lie back and go to sleep again.'

But I couldn't go to sleep, I couldn't. She must have known that, I thought irritably. I tried to tell her what I wanted with my eyes. I looked at her pleadingly, passionately, begging her to answer my unformed question. For a few moments she stood looking down at me, a puzzled line creasing her forehead. Then she seemed to understand.

She gave a wide, reassuring smile.

'Now, don't you worry. You've had a nasty shock. Some madman tried to strangle you. Your neck's been cut about a bit ... But there's nothing permanently damaged. A week or two here and we'll be able to pack you off home.'

I looked at her dumbly. I felt as if I were about to tumble over the edge of a terrifying precipice, which I had climbed painfully and laboriously. I motioned her nearer, struggling to speak. The words came out at last, each one hurting the dry swollen lining of my throat.

'Please,' I said, 'Please bring a mirror.'

The nurse hesitated, then nodded. She went over to the corner and came back holding a large oval hand mirror.

'There you are,' she said soothingly, 'Only some bandages around your neck. Nothing very frightening, is it?'

But I didn't answer her. I looked in the mirror and the face I saw was a familiar one. It was small and ugly with protruding teeth and sunken eyes, and the head was bald and round, like a bullet.

III

The Happiest Day of Their Lives

'All right,' she said. 'I'll marry you.'
There had been difficulties. Their parents had thought they were still too young though, as they pointed out, they were surely old enough to know their own minds. In the end, somewhat grudgingly, consent had been given and they had been married quietly at the local registry office, leaving soon afterwards for a honeymoon at the other end of Wales, in a small fishing village in Carmarthenshire.

It had been as simple as that. Alan had made all the travel arrangements. He was like that, careful and practical, a bit of a worrier, perhaps, but at least someone who took action and got things done.

She supposed that must have been what had drawn her to him in the first place. It had been refreshing for someone as vague as herself to be taken in charge of and organised, so that there was really nothing left to worry about.

She smiled wryly. Perhaps that was not quite the way to phrase things. There was, in fact, a great deal to worry about. The next twenty-four hours, for instance, was not merely a question of just another passage of time. It was likely to be a turning point – in her own life, and in his, too.

She sat back in the taxi carrying them to the station and studied his face as he sat beside her, gazing thoughtfully out of the side window. Young though she was herself, only just twenty, she suddenly felt quite grown up while he – he looked almost a babe, the down still soft on his cheek ... She smiled to herself secretively at the idea, knowing how cross he would have been if he had guessed what she was thinking.

'What is it?' he said suddenly, turning.

'Nothing ...'

He smiled, and suddenly took her hand and pressed it gently.

'Don't worry. Everything will be all right.'

The funny thing was that though she didn't for a moment believe in the easy promise of his words she did derive great comfort from his presence. It had always been like that: he had given her reassurance and stability – not by anything he did or said but by his own curiously rock-like presence.

It wasn't so much an outward thing – physically he was slightly built, almost frail, though his features were firmly and strongly drawn. No, it was some kind of inner quality, she supposed. Yet even as she supposed that, almost by instinct she put up a hand and ran a finger gently down the softness of his cheek – a gesture of tenderness she found herself quite unable to resist.

He said nothing, but after a moment put up his own hand and touched the back of her palm gently so that for a moment it was as if the two of them were welded together in some mysterious communion.

They sat there like that, enclosed within a kind of cocoon of happiness, for the rest of the taxi journey to the station. And once there, all the time he was off buying the tickets, she stood waiting with their two rather new suitcases, still somehow lost in a kind of dream world – looking, a detached observer might well have thought, like any young lover waiting for her love.

When they were safely settled in an empty compartment near the front of the train he took hold of her left hand and bent forward, examining it carefully. Then with a shy sort of smile that touched her heart, he said:

'I'm sorry it's not a diamond or something.'

She looked rather blankly at the smooth ring which now adorned her fourth finger, transforming her officially and for the benefit of inquisitive landladies and suchlike into a legally accredited wife.

Was it really as simple as all that, she wondered just fitting a piece of metal over one finger, did it really make all that difference? Change you from a gangling teenager into a respectable married woman? Was that really possible?

She tried to concentrate on the problem during the long winding journey through valleys and mountains, past lush hills and waterfalls, and then at last out into the openness and, beyond, the sea coast ... But somehow the solution eluded her. She only knew that in some curious way she felt her life bound up with this tense very youthful looking man at her side, and that whatever else happened he had only to turn and look at her with his dark limpid eyes and it was as if he saw into her very heart ... leaving her limp and trembling.

It had been this sense of the inevitability of their relationship, she supposed, that persuaded her into the adventure of their early marriage and the away from it all honeymoon at the tiny Welsh fishing village which waited at the end of their journey. Every time they were together, every time she turned wordlessly to him and he took her into his arms and held her so tightly she could hardly breathe nor wanted to ... it was a kind of torture.

'Darling,' he would whisper in her ear. 'Darling, darling ... I want you so.'

It wasn't just him, either. She must be honest. Whatever strange feelings possessed him she knew they were reciprocated in the secret recesses of her own being. It had been her idea as much as his that they should take the decisive, even perhaps dangerous step. She smiled, watching Alan as he stepped on to the platform ahead of her, as he did so seeming in that anonymous setting at once to become himself almost a stranger – she began to feel afraid.

It was a feeling that pursued her, disturbingly, for the remainder of the short journey from the small station down the cobbled hill to the huddled boarding houses around the harbour. By the time they reached the one where Alan had booked, this unease, far from vanishing, had grown alarmingly.

'For goodness sake,' whispered Alan, half way up the path. 'Don't hang back like that. It looks – odd.'

It was the first time he had ever spoken to her so sharply,

but she hardly noticed. She was too occupied in fighting down the feeling of utter panic which swept over her as she stood awkwardly, clasping both suitcases as if for comfort, while Alan rang the bell.

Actually the woman who answered the door was rather nice, in a homely way. She made them welcome, insisted on carrying one of the cases and showed them with obvious pride into what was probably her best bedroom, looking over the harbour.
'You'll be hungry after such a long journey. Well, there's some supper for you downstairs when you're ready.'
Then she was gone, and the girl realised that for the first time, left alone with Alan, she felt awkward. She crossed to the window and looked out upon the little harbour, the tiny blue and white boats bobbing about like little corks, the fisherman's cottages huddling around like doll's houses. It all looked neat and tidy and natural. She had to force herself to turn back upon the strange, rather anonymous view of the bedroom.
'Well ...' she said.
Alan, sitting awkwardly on the edge of the bed, looked up.
'Yes?'
She forced a smile.
'Well ... here we are.'
He made a vague gesture.
'I suppose we ought to unpack.'
She hesitated.
'No,' she said. 'Not now – let's – let's go and eat, like she said.'

The meal was served in a small rather formal dining room, which obviously during the holiday season would hold about a dozen people. Now being the only couple, they were each a little self-conscious, as if spotlighted on a stage. Each time the woman brought a plate of something Alan thanked her overelaborately: then, in the same stilted tones he would turn to the girl and ask her if she wanted the salt, or the pepper, or something else. If it hadn't all been so depressing the girl would have wanted to burst into laughter. As it was, she was not far from tears.

When the coffee came at the end of the meal the landlady obviously felt justified in indulging in a little chat. Politely they joined in, asking the expected questions. Yes, replied the landlady, it was quiet now, yes, in the season it was very busy indeed. But of course this time of the year they had very few visitors – only honeymoon couples, like themselves.

This, obviously was the cue for some delicate probing of their own affairs. The girl could see that Alan was flustered out of his usual composure. Loyally she tried to back him up with irrelevant descriptions of their courtship and wedding day. In an odd way the sharing of this experience made her feel close to Alan for the first time since they had come. But then she felt deflated again when the woman said with a kindly nod.

'Ah well, I'm sure you'll be very happy – very happy indeed.'

They went for a walk after supper. She had hoped somehow that strolling along, talking together, they would break the sense of unease. But somehow it was not like that.

'I didn't expect,' she said, trying to explain. 'To feel so – so – well, strange. Maybe it's something to do with the landlady – it's almost as if we weren't married or something.'

'I don't know why you say that,' he said defensively. 'We are married – and anyway I'm sure the landlady doesn't think any different.'

She looked at him doubtfully.

'You're just being silly – ' he said, almost petulantly.

She shrugged.

'I'm sorry, Alan.'

They went down to the harbour wall and sat watching the peaceful scene. It was all quite as romantic and away-from-it-all as they had planned. And yet ...

Troubled, she put out a hand and found his.

'I'm really sorry, darling.'

He squeezed her, happy in the simple response.

'So am I.'

It was nearly dark when they returned to the boarding house. They said an awkward goodnight to the landlady and went up stairs to their bedroom. When they went in she had hoped they would be greeted by a romantic view out upon the harbour ... instead the curtains were firmly drawn and the room brightly illuminated by electric light.

'Oh,' exclaimed the girl in dismay. She sat on the bed wearily, feeling like crying. As she did so she was vaguely aware of Alan wandering around the room uneasily.

'For goodness sake,' she said at last, irritably. 'Stop mooning around.'

They undressed quietly and quickly, with their backs to each other. By the time he had finished she was already in bed, the sheets pulled up to her chin. She watched the uneasy movements with which finally he lifted the bedclothes and slid in beside her, careful to keep some distance ... and she wondered why on earth she should feel so alien.

It was a little better when he put out the light, and the room was faintly illuminated by lights from the harbour. After a while his hand stretched out, feeling for hers.

'It isn't quite as we planned, is it.'

'No.' She wanted to say something else, but couldn't find the words.

As if feeling the same bereftness of communication he turned to her suddenly and, almost desperately, took her in his arms.

'Darling ...'

Whatever her mind might have willed, her body gave its answer in an immediate stiffening, and gently she pushed him away.

'Alan ... I'm sorry ... but ...' She shook her head, not far from tears in the gathering darkness. 'I can't, I just can't ...'

After a while he removed his arm from her shoulder and lay back, so that their two bodies, though side by side, were not touching. She had not understood before the pain of lying so close together, and yet so far apart ... but there seemed nothing she could do about it. She supposed they could have talked, but there seemed nothing to say. It was, after all, their honeymoon night; and this was her husband, lying silently beside her; and yet she felt strangely withdrawn, imprisoned by the walls of her own unexpected reticence.

Like that, she fell gradually into an uneasy slumber in which it seemed as if she became detached from her body like some lost spirit floating through some enormous void. Just when she was beginning to feel a little lost and afraid she was jerked into wakefulness by someone pulling at her shoulders.

'Wake up,' he whispered.

It was still the strange half light before dawn, and in the dimness she made out his face looking down upon her eagerly.

'It's almost dawn. What do you say to our getting up and having an early swim?'

As if in a dream she nodded, and followed his example in clambering out of bed and dressing quietly so as to wake no one else. Then grabbing costume and towel, she followed him downstairs and out into the strange white morning air.

'Look!' He pointed, beyond the harbour to the humped cliffs. 'There are sand-dunes and a beach further on, I noticed them yesterday when we drove in. Come on, it'll be marvellous.'

Funnily enough, as they hurried along the cobbled streets and then out on to the cliff path that led over the hill and down to the sand-dunes, she found it *was* all rather marvellous. By now the sun had peeped over the horizon and its slanting fresh rays glistened on the sea and touched the sandy beach with the new day's radiance. Now that they had climbed over the hill there was not a building in sight, not another human being in existence.

'Oh, Alan,' she cried out in sudden happiness. 'I'm glad we came.'

They undressed quickly behind one of the sand-dunes and then, holding hands, raced down the sloping sands towards the white lipped line of waiting water. The sea was cold and clear, and at the first shock of its touch they gasped and shrieked ... but soon they adjusted themselves, and began swimming. They were both good swimmers, but this was the first time they had been to the sea together, and in some subtle way they were aware of the importance of this first shared new experience.

'Race you to that rock over there,' called out Alan.

'All right,' she spluttered.

They swam side by side, hardly racing really, but enjoying the act of swimming together. Somehow they managed to reach the craggy rock at the same time: Alan pulled himself up and then held out a hand and half dragged her out of the water. He grinned.

'We're the kings of the castle!'

When they had got their breath back, they swam back to the shore, then lay on their backs splashing about lazily. Already the sun had risen quite a way so that they could feel its warmth, but it was still early and everything around was silent and sleeping.

'Oh, Alan,' she said, half laughing still, with her arm round his waist in almost unconscious affection. 'This is heavenly.'

Still exhilarated by this feeling she followed him out of the sea and up to the sand-dunes where they had left their clothes. They had undressed in such a hurry that she had hardly noticed the process, but now, as they sank down on the sands side by side she wondered if she might feel a sudden sense of awkwardness. Instead, it all seemed easy and familiar, as if they had been companions for ever and ever.

'Oh, Alan,' she said, lifting her head and throwing back her damp hair. 'That was wonderful ... wonderful ...'

Almost without thinking she began to unloosen the straps of her bathing costume ... hesitated, momentarily, as if aware of his sudden stillness beside her ... and then, blushing faintly, slipped the straps off and pulled the costume down.

When she felt his hands, hot and moist, suddenly touching her shoulders and then more urgently pulling her down towards him she had no more hesitation or doubts or conjectures ... she was aware only of the blue sky opening out above, of the bright morning sun beating down so warm and ardent – yet not one half as warm and ardent as this young and marvellous sun-god of her own, whose radiance now was all about her, enveloping and enfolding her more completely, more marvellously, than all the dawns in history.

'Darling ...' he whispered. 'My very own darling ... I love you ... more than anything else in the world.'

And all at once, there in the secret other world of the lonely sand-dunes, everything was honeysuckle and roses and fragrant perfumes and the promise of more and more wonders, enhanced and illuminated, and above all enriched by a new found tenderness of which neither of them could ever have been aware before.

'My love,' she thought, transfixed. 'Oh, my love!'

It was still comparatively early when they made their way back to the little boarding house by the harbour. Just a few old fishermen were up and about, mending nets and preparing boats for their inevitable journeys. They nodded cheerful good mornings and the girl held Alan's arm more tightly and went with him back into the boarding house. The landlady heard them come in but wisely kept out of the way ... a little while later however she came to the bottom of the stairs and called out cheerfully, 'Breakfast's ready!'

And soon they came down the stairs arm in arm, bringing with them a curious new radiance of happiness so that it would have been difficult indeed for anyone to dispute that it was indeed the happiest day of their lives.

IV

The Woman Who Walked Away

The woman was thirty-eight, dark-haired, sleepy-eyed, a big woman whose height saved her from being plump and lent to her heavy movements a certain sensual grace. For ten years she had lived in a suburban semi-detached house with her husband, and their two small children. Every morning she made breakfast of tea and toast and fried egg and bacon for her husband, helped him on with his coat and duly waved him goodbye on his way to catch the 8.36 train into the city. A little afterwards she dressed her children for their journey by bus to a nearby preparatory school. When they were gone she tidied away the breakfast things, swept out the rooms, made the beds, and came downstairs into the kitchen. There she sat down at the scrubbed table and looked around the spick and span room, its order, its neatness – its barrenness. She was aware, unbearably, of her boredom; her utter and complete boredom.

Always the feeling had been there, but lately it had grown upon her like some festering sore. Now its impact was continual and terrible. It followed her about like some unwanted leper that she could not be rid of – it was not a bad condition or aspect of her life, it *was* her life. Bored. Bored, bored with her husband. Bored with her children. Bored with her home, bored with the whole routine of her existence. Bored with herself.

And as the feeling grew, as each day she gave herself up a little more to her *malaise*, so its description began to seem quite inadequate. Boredom was a nonentity of a word to express, what she felt. Distaste, disinterest, dissatisfaction – none of these vague words could sum up the things that festered and burned inside her. Burned, indeed! – she could almost feel the hotness and flames within her body, so that she could not sit still for long but must be moving about restlessly, upstairs and downstairs, wandering into rooms, staring out of windows, waiting for what she did not know ... One day it occurred to her that she had underestimated the feeling, the whole business. Hate was a better word; a cleaner word. Hatred. Awful, consuming hatred. Hate for Henry, hate for the children. Hate for the walls which they had created around her. Hate for the prison she had created for herself.

That day was an important one for her. It marked a change in the processes. She became aware of the possibility of action, even of violence. It was not enough to sit at the kitchen table, aching with the intolerable burden of emptiness. Indeed, it could not be enough; sooner or later she would go mad at such an impasse.

One morning in the kitchen, staring upon the oil-checked table, she became aware of her empty, craving hands. She held them before her eyes, bewildered, frustrated. She felt in them their impotence, their desire to do something, anything, to cause something to happen. She placed them on the table, took hold of the oil cloth, and with a savage movement ripped it into two pieces.

Later in the day she picked up an old cane chair and broke it into pieces, banging it relentlessly against the stone floor, savouring each splintering sound and crackle. It was strange, the ecstasy of the feeling, the exquisite release. She had to restrain herself from other acts of violence, from tearing at curtains, from attacking the furniture. She was aware of urges within her; boiling, seething urges to destroy, to obliterate these vestiges of her awful, boring life.

That night, when her husband came home, she considered him dispassionately: his face, his figure, his manner, his utter familiarity. He was meaningless to her. She loved not him, but herself. Everything else was meaningless, a pretence. The whole ten years had been a pretence. She had pretended even to herself, that she cared about him. It was a lie. Secretly, always, she had cared only about herself, what she felt, her sensations. But she had been afraid to admit it, afraid.

His pomposity! His petulance! His meanness! His schoolmaster's turn of phrase, his narrowness, his lack of imagination. How had she stood it so long? Why? His very presence – lean and stringy, bent-shouldered – it was an offence to her. His body – how could she have borne his body, his hands, his carefully manicured nails? How could she have borne to let him touch her, stroke her, make love to her? At the mere thought she winced with pain, her face convulsed with delayed suffering and distaste. And that very night, as if sensing her restlessness for the first time, her husband embarked on his futile overtures. He patted her shoulder, he kissed her brow, he slid his arm around her waist. He made some heavy joke about the bedroom, about bed. He looked at her expectantly, his spectacled eyes gleaming like a little boy's.

So she hit him. She hit him with all her force, all her power, all her seething rage – a wild, hurtful blow, across the face, so vivid and savage that she could feel the pain in each finger of the hand.

It almost knocked him over. He staggered back, bewildered. She did not move. She stood watching him, as if she watched some film, some passing scene. He looked at her in confusion. He took a step towards her. She hit him again, this time with such force that her knuckles drew blood.

He staggered across the room, looking at her wildly. 'What – I don't – ?'

But she did not move. She felt strangely, magnificently detached. He was not her husband, he was a pompous old man, a fool, a stupid idiot. All her hatred was concentrated into the two blows; with them she felt conscious of wiping him out of her life, even as she had broken the chair, ripped the table cloth. She was aware in that moment that she would have done the same to anything, even to the children. She could have hated and destroyed them, had they stood in her way, so all-consuming was her need to be free, to break the awful, consuming weight, the imprisonment, of her ten years of boredom.

After that it was a question of time; her next action, the step after that, and the one after that. She could not bear him near her, she would not even speak to him. The children found her remote, she found them unreal. The house was like a paper building. She had the feeling that with scissors or a match, or a strong puff of breath, she could destroy it for ever. Perhaps, perhaps ...?

One morning when her husband had gone to work, when her children had gone to school – when she had made the beds, and tidied the rooms – she walked out of the house. She went out to buy some groceries; in the main street she had the sudden foreknowledge of no return; on her way back she got a bus, a bus going south, into the country.

In the bus, rolling over pleasant green land, she was aware of her composure, her coolness. I have never really been alive, she thought. She looked down at her ordinary suburban dress, her mass-produced shoes, her shiny handbag. They were all she possessed and she hated them for what they represented. She wanted to be free of them, free of everything; just herself, her body, alone with the world, alone and free. She looked out of the window at the tawny slopes of a heath, at the boughs of the trees bending beneath the wind, at bushes rustling and shivering at the wind's touch. She imagined herself there, running across the heath, kissed by the wind, ravished by the sun. Awake, awake, awake! I have never really been alive, she thought.

The bus took her down to the sea, down to the tang of seaweed and the salty air. She got out in the antiseptic white-washed centre of a modern bus station. Around her people were coming and going, coming and going. She looked in her handbag. She had a five pound note and some small change. What shall I do? she thought. Where shall I go? The questions seemed curiously unimportant. She walked out of the bus station and across a wide road to the promenade. There was the sea, blue and gleaming, the horizon inviting. She began walking along the promenade, her handbag swinging, her money jinkling. I am rich, she thought. I am rich, rich. She felt the sun on her face, the sweetness in her breath. And in truth as she walked there was a new buoyancy, her body was lithe and vibrant, she held herself as if on air, as if in joy.

She walked a long way. When she felt tired she sat on the wall of the promenade, staring at the waves, at the wet pebbles, at distant smoke. When she felt hot and thirsty she crossed the road and went into the little ice cream parlour. She ordered a huge ice cream sundae, strawberry and vanilla and coffee, covered with a great blob of cream. She stared greedily at the cream, the colours. She spooned a huge heap into her mouth, feeling the cold shock of it, savouring its sweetness. She wanted to enjoy everything, to savour everything. She stared around the cafe avidly, reading every notice, every silly notice. Her eyes met the proprietor's, a bald-headed man leaning nonchalantly across the counter. He looked at her with surprise. She felt she wanted to fondle his bald head, to stroke his neat moustache. She smiled, she giggled, she was highly amused. Perturbed he came over and stood by her, fat and gross, sweaty, yet infinitely preferable to her unlamented husband.

'Is anything the matter, madam?'

No, nothing is the matter, madam. Yes, something is the matter, madam. Secretly she repeated words to herself; phrases, whole paragraphs of nonsense. She felt hilariously, wonderfully, gay. She could do anything, she could achieve anything. She smiled at him, her lips wide, richly red, her teeth white, her tongue dancing. She laughed at him.

'I'd like to stroke your moustache!'

She laughed again, and paid her bill and went out, leaving him perturbed. He did not like women who laughed. You never were safe with them ...

She did not want to be safe. Never again. She wanted the uncertain, the unknown, the magic.

That's it, she thought. That's what it is. It is all there, waiting. If I walk far enough, if I explore, if I search.

The sea became greyer, the promenade a street. Cement

poles marked the trolley bus lines. She came into the outer environs of a town, a dockyard port, a big sprawling place. She moved now among tall buildings, grey tenements. The air was less pleasant, the afternoon strident with traffic and buses, with hurrying people. In the distance she saw the cranes, the peep of red funnels; now and then a tug hooted, a ship replied.

She was tired now. She saw a grimy house, a notice in the window. ACCOMMODATION. She knocked at the door. A slut of an old woman, white-haired like a crone, peeped from behind the door.

'What is it?'

'I want a room.'

The crone looked doubtful.

'There's mostly sailors here.'

She laughed.

'I don't mind. I like sailors.'

'Well, there's a room at the top.'

It was indeed at the top. Five flights up. Just an attic-room; just a bed, a washbowl, a stand, an old painting of Jesus Christ. And a window looking out on the railway. Not even the sea. But she took it. She felt curiously at home.

It was a pound a night. She took it for two nights. She felt that was all the insurance she could allow herself. The crone took the money in advance. Then she shuffled away, taking with her the smell of tobacco, beer, dusty faded roses, a curious memory of the sea, perhaps of sailors.

In the evening the woman went out again. It was nearly dusk. The lights began to shine, even the dour industrial streets took on a fairy-like quality. Passing among them the woman felt ready for magic and adventure. There was something in her look, something in her vivacity, something in her walk ...

A big car drew up just past her. She walked towards it confidently. A man's voice inquired, a little uncertainly: 'Are you going this way?'

The woman smiled. The car was a carriage, the man a prince.

'I'm going any way, all ways. Isn't it a wonderful evening?'

She got into the car and sat beside him. The seat was luxuriously soft, she sank deep into it, watching the man's expert movements as he started up, changed gear, soared the car forward. It seemed like floating on air.

'My husband was too mean to buy a car.'

The man turned towards her, uncertain.

'Your husband ...?'

The woman smiled, teeth gleaming, eyes alight.

'I have no husband ...'

The man smiled. He was dark, good-looking, with a hat pulled low over his forehead. He was a commercial traveller, a book-keeper, a shop owner, a manager, a company director, a hotel manager, a bookmaker, an engineer – no matter, he was a prince.

He drove the car to the town centre, to a huge hotel. They went into the smart cocktail bar. The woman was no longer conscious of her shabby clothes. Somehow she transcended them. She was aglow with her own life. She laughed and chattered, her eyes flashed, her lips pouted. The man could hardly believe his luck. He did not see her age, her ten years, her memories. He saw only her life.

After several drinks he took her upstairs to his room. It was a room, like all the other sixty-four rooms in the hotel, but to the woman it was a room apart, a palace, a gold room, a queenly boudoir. She waltzed around, admiring the extravagant lines of the dressing table, the huge walnut wardrobe, the ankle long mirror. In front of the mirror she paused, examining herself critically, soulfully.

The man came up behind her. He put his arms on her shoulders. Under his grip he could feel her warm flesh, her beating pulse, her fierce life. He became caught in her own magic, woven into the pattern of some mysterious tapestry. He undid the buttons at the back of the dress. He pulled it down over her shoulders. He let the dress drop to the ground and began undoing the straps of the woman's brassiere. Then he undressed her completely, not taking his eyes the whole time from the mirror and the woman's face.

'You're beautiful,' said the man, fondling her back, her breasts her thighs. 'You're wonderful. You're beautiful.'

I am, thought the woman. I am, I am, I am! And she thought bitterly of the ten years of waste, the ten years of vegetation.

The bed was covered with a silver-tinted quilt. The woman lay upon it like some goddess. The man was amazed, startled, uplifted. His hands burned to touch her. His eyes devoured her beauty. His heart beat with a wild thump as he made love to her, roused her, fought fiercely before drowning in the wild seas of the unrestrained, frightening passion.

It was over soon. The man lay back on the bed, confused, breathless; exhilarated and yet despondent. He knew he had made fleeting contact with something he would not easily forget.

He held his hands towards the woman. She smiled into his face. She leaned her big body over him for her breasts to touch him gently. Then, even as he caressed her, she melted away. He watched her walk about the room, her whiteness swimming before his eyes. What was the matter? Where was she going? Why did she leave him?

The woman opened the window and let in the night air, the moon, the stars.

'See! The world outside. Isn't it wonderful?'

'YOU are wonderful,' said the man breathlessly. 'I don't know ... I mean ... Did you ...?'

But even as he spoke, this pleasant, charming, but rather seedy man with caution in his eyes and a thinning head, the woman began to vanish. It seemed to him that in a moment she had dressed herself, had flung her clothes about her magnificent body as if they were rags.

'But I say – look here – I – ?'

She stood in the doorway, remote, unreal. She blew him a kiss.

'Good-bye!'

She was gone.

It was still early evening. The woman walked along the main

street, past the shining shop windows. She felt exhilaration in her bones. She felt young. She warmed at the thought of the man's caresses, the touch of his flesh, the excitement of lovemaking. She wanted to make love to the whole world, the whole gorgeous world. She was possessed with lust, greed, avidness. Her husband would not have known her.

Before the bright lights of the dance-hall she paused, and went in. The sound of music floated up to greet her. She let it penetrate into her being, like the day, the wind, the sea, the love-making. She wanted to assimilate everything, every moment every experience. Swaying gently as she walked she entered the dance-hall, the smoke and the sweat and the downbeat of the band. In no time she was whirled away on someone's arms, whirled round and round, under the gay lights and the hollow ceiling. She smiled at each partner, at each new face. She liked all the faces, all the bodies that pressed against her. She liked all men, all life. She was alive, alive, alive.

At the end of the dance the woman emerged on the arm of a burly docker. He was an immensely strong man, whose strength almost burst through his check shirt. The woman was fascinated by his gleaming muscles, his iron-hard chest, his pulsating vigour. She clung to his arm contentedly while he led her down into the dark mysteries of the dock. He was a poor man, she knew from the way he talked and thought. He lived sparsely, frugally, he had a wife and three children. But he was starved of something as she was starved of something. Something beyond wife, children, conventions – something of freedom, abandonment.

He took her into the shadows of a bomb site. There were the remains of a room, the walls still standing. Grass had grown miraculously in a corner. Neither of them spoke. The big man lifted her up like a child. In his arms she felt deliciously weak. He pressed her body against his, close, closer. Her arms crept under his shirt, fondling his flesh, the hairs, the sweat, the hard muscles. Together they sank on to the grass. They were lost, lost, lost, deep into the pool of passion.

Passion, thought the woman. Passion, passion, passion! It

was like the air, like food, like wine. She would never tire of it. She had never known what it could be like. She gripped the man fiercely. She bit into his shoulder, his back. Her fingers clawed at him with tender fierceness until he gasped. Their love-making seemed endless, cruel, wild, wonderful.

Later the woman walked back alone to her room. She felt quiet and calm, like a lake that had suddenly become undisturbed. She felt an immense content, as of the mountaineer that has climbed the peak, the painter that has completed the picture. She felt dizzy, tired, weak. Alone, thankfully, richly, beautifully alone. And alive.

She let herself in and crept up the stairs to her haven at the top. She was glad to undress in darkness, to slip into bed, to fall into deep untroubled sleep. She slept without remorse, with pleasure, a smile at her lips. And even as she slept life flared through her like fire, storing and renewing.

When she awoke, in the morning, she slipped a coat over her nakedness and went to the bathroom below. As she came out she saw a sailor standing in the doorway of the room opposite. A boy almost, a boy with blue eyes and fair hair, and a curving mouth, a schoolboy grin. He looked fresh and clean and wild. His eyes were bright as they stared right through her coat, so that she might never have been wearing it. The woman's breath hissed through her lips. She felt herself quiver with hotness as she met the sailor's eyes. She went upstairs into her room. She half closed the door behind her, and went to her bed. When she took the coat off and turned, the sailor was standing in the doorway. He was young and beautiful, so fair and fresh that the woman felt like she had bathed in some glorious sea.

It was like that for a week. The woman felt born again. She had no hesitations, no doubts, no recriminations. She knew herself to be free of all those things, to be as the leaf in the wind. She belonged to no one. She gave her body to men because she wanted them, she needed them, all their bizarre experiences, all their secret lives and hopes, all their consummating manhood. She was carried by them through a sexual world of experience that lifted her up, transformed her.

The Woman Who Walked Away 69

It took ten years off her life.

At the end of the week she left the town. She walked out of the town as she had walked in, with her two strong feet, her body firm and graceful, her spirit burning unquenched. She walked out into the green fields and the golden lanes. The sun greeted her from behind a cloud. The world was ever beautiful. Life was rich and endless. She had no thought of her husband, her children, her past. They did not exist. Now was the only existence.

A lorry gave her a lift. And then another. A farmer in a shooting brake picked her up. They had lunch in a wayside pub. Afterwards he drove on, stopped by a thick wood. He suggested they take a stroll. They passed through the darkness into a sunlit glade. He looked at her with burning eyes. Silently she undid her dress. Murmuring softly, he took hold of her, shook her clothes away, caressed her rich whiteness in the burning sunlight.

She did not mind. That was her secret. She minded nothing. She cared about nothing. She accepted everything. All pleasure was her pleasure. All pain was her pain. She feared nothing, there was nothing to fear. She desired everything, then all was desire. She was utterly given up to the moment, the golden moment.

She passed on her way, unknown, unheralded – unforgettable. She was like a butterfly; fluttering along the lanes, between the honeysuckles and the thyme. She shone and glowed in the very light towards which she travelled, for she carried with her the lustre of her uprising, her outbreak, her tremendous rebellion. At her passage the air seemed to rustle, wings to flutter. She was a sight to behold; men turned and watched her and she was like some image of their imagination, some consummation of their desire. She passed on her way like some sinewy flame; hay barns, lofts, cottages, farms, manors, castles. All were her abodes, reverberating at her coming and going. Love was her passage. Like war, she threaded relentlessly through villages and towns, sowing seed where she passed; of destruction, of creation.

One evening many weeks later, walking along a country

lane, the woman saw ahead the winding smoke of a gipsy encampment. There was a caravan parked in a small opening, and a tent beside it. A fire burned outside the tent, and two children gathered around it. They were kindling the sticks, heartening the fire to boil a pot of stew. The woman stood and watched, in silence, the dirty children in their tattered clothes, the grey tent, the faded caravan, the flickering fire. It was like a scene from a picture, but she was suddenly, subtly, a part of it.

The children did not see the woman. But an old gipsy sitting on the steps of the caravan looked up and saw her. And at his look she advanced slowly into the encampment.

'Welcome,' said the old gipsy. He was a small man, with a red scarf round his head, and wise eyes. The woman liked him.

'Will you eat with us?'

'Yes,' said the woman. 'I will be glad to eat with you.'

The children turned to her then. They had bright mischievous eyes, they were like little animals. Soon they romped and played. The woman bent down and caught them in her arms, like fluff. They shrieked their delight.

The woman put them down suddenly. She got to her feet. A man stood behind her.

'This is my eldest son,' said the old gipsy. 'His name is Andrea.'

The woman turned. It was the man in the car, the docker, the young sailor, the farmer, all the others. And something beyond. Something quite beyond and apart. The end of a journey.

'Hello, Andrea,' she said.

The man was dark and sinewy, with bright beady eyes, a lean jaw, an almost cruel face. He wore green corduroy trousers and a khaki shirt. His head was bare, the hair dark and curled; he wore golden earrings. He was the woman's age, he was the woman's man.

'We are nomads,' said Andrea. 'We travel the country. We have no home. We eat off what we can find, what we can sell. My mother is dead. My father is very old, he cannot do much.

I have to care for him, for my little brother and sister.'

'I will care for them,' said the woman simply. Her voice dropped into intimacy. 'And for you.'

'Come,' called the old man, 'Supper is ready. Let us eat.'

They ate round the fire, from the pot of stewed rabbit. They ate steadily and in silence. The children had another helping. Then it was time for them to go to bed. The woman went with them into the tent. She undressed their sinewy little bodies, she fondled them gently before tucking their warmth under the blanket. Then she sang them a song, a song she had never heard before, that seemed to come naturally to her lips. When she had finished singing the children were asleep.

When the woman came out of the tent the old man had gone. Andrea sat cross-legged by the fire. She sat down beside him.

'The fire is warm,' said Andrea. 'I like warmth.'

'Fire is life,' said the woman. 'Life is warmth. I hate the cold and the ugly, the prim and the prude.'

Andrea looked upwards.

'There are stars in the sky. A thousand stars, but only one moon. I am attracted to all the stars, but I belong to the moon.'

'I am the moon,' said the woman softly. 'I am the sun and the moon.'

Andrea looked at her in the flickering firelight.

'I believe you.'

They went for a walk. Down bracken strewn paths, between honeysuckled lanes. It was still and silent, save for the hoots of owls, the call of rooks. They were miles from cities, from towns, from suburban streets.

'We are alone in the universe,' said Andrea. 'Our lives are in the palms of our hands. We make our own journey, or it is made for us. We seek our own ends or they are ordained for us.'

'We only live once,' said the woman.

'It is the life we choose.'

'It is important how we choose.'

'You are beautiful in the firelight,' said the gipsy.

'You are beautiful in the dark,' said the woman.

She felt with her hand for the curly dark hair upon his head, and twined her fingers between its roughness.

'You are beautiful to me,' she said softly, 'because I have looked for you so long.'

They were silent then. The night was all around them. The stars winked and twinkled like naughty fairies. But the moon hung low and luminous, like eternal love.

'We shall live hardly,' said Andrea. 'No man will make us welcome. No place will hold us for long. Our home will be on the road, our roof the sky. We shall be poor and often hungry. The future will always be uncertain. You must know all these things.'

'We shall have love,' said the woman, 'and kindness and cruelty, passion and pity, hardness and softness. I desire you in all those ways, and many other secret ways.'

The gipsy held her in his arms. He did not speak of his desire, it was written in his eyes, communicated in his touch, spoken of in his breath.

The woman laughed, her laugh ringing all around, in the woods, in the air, in the world.

Without a word the gipsy picked her up and carried her back to the caravan. Their bed was made of bracken. Their pillow was grass. Their night was of darkness and mystery and magic. In the morning the sun shone upon their happiness.

And in the morning the caravan moved on. They followed their horse, they followed the road. They wandered on, up hill and down hill, over the unending country. Nobody knew where they came from, nobody knew where they went. They were as children of the darkness, except that they were children of the light. They had few possessions, only the clothes they stood in, they seldom knew where their next meal would come from. But they lived with the sun and the moon and the stars.

One day they came to a town. The gipsy had carved strips of wood into pegs. The woman carried a bag full of these and called down a row of neat red-brick houses. It was a tidy, uniform, anonymous suburban road. She knocked at the door of each house and offered her wares. Sometimes they were bought, sometimes refused.

At one door the woman had a strange feeling. Have I been here before, she wondered? Is this the world I used to inhabit? It might have been, it might not have been. She could no longer be sure.

The lady of the house answered the door. She had mouse-coloured hair pushed back into a bun. She looked rather tired. Her face was drawn into a tight rash of petulance. Her eyes were dull and incurious. She wore a conventional blue dress.

'Would you like some pegs?' said the woman.

'Well, I haven't much money. I must be careful. How much are they?'

But the woman did not hear. She was staring past the other. She saw the kitchen, neat and orderly. She saw the gleaming stove, the tidy shelves. She saw the empty table, with its smooth oil-cloth. And she remembered everything, all that she had tried to forget.

'Here!' cried the woman, in an ecstasy of pity, a torrent of sadness. 'Have them for nothing. They are free – take them, my friend. Take them, oh my poor sister.'

And she turned and left the other standing perplexed with a bunch of wooden pegs in her hand.

'Well!' exclaimed the lady of the house, and she retreated into her cage and shut the door upon herself.

But the woman walked on without looking back. She sang as she strode down the street, in her tattered clothes and her worn rope sandals. She sang and she smiled as she walked away down the suburban street.

She was one in a million.

V

The Surfer

Mr Pemberton came upon surfing, as in fact we usually come upon the great revelations of life, in an accidental sort of way. Up to that moment he had been almost a model of sober propriety, a solid, well-set up young man with aspirations to be something in the city. Along with a few million others he had caught his regular morning train from the suburbs, spent his quota of somewhat dull hours totting up figures, and sometimes dividing them again, and in general dutifully followed the somewhat uneventful career which his parents, if perhaps not nature, had mapped out for him.

It wasn't very exciting, let's be honest. It was hardly, shall we say, an exhilarating sort of prospect. All the same probably Mr Pemberton would have continued cutting for himself one of those familiar, and indeed quite comfortable ruts – if there had not been somewhere deep inside him, one of those tiny voices, those little rebellious streaks which, fortunately, haunt a good many human beings. The sort of niggling pinprick which sometimes made young Mr Pemberton stop in his tracks when walking beside the Embankment to stare wistfully at some sea-bound tanker puffing off to unknown horizons – or caused him to emerge from some enthralling adventure film fiercely twirling his rolled up umbrella preparatory to taking on a gang of bandits.

At least, one must assume it was something like this which brought surfing to Mr Pemberton – or to be more accurate, gave Mr Pemberton to surfing.

It happened one holiday-time when Mr Pemberton, for want of any more specific plan, had accompanied a party of men friends on a motoring tour of Cornwall. Like most visitors to that Western tip of our islands Mr Pemberton was suitably impressed by the majestic moorlands and the rugged cliffs: but that might have been the end of matters, had it not been for that quite casual visit, one sunny but blustery afternoon, to a certain holiday resort along the North Cornwall coast. It was there, strolling along the wide sandy front, that Mr Pemberton chanced to look curiously seawards and perceive in their full fury and splendour, those legendary Atlantic rollers, pounding and sweeping over the glistening golden sands. Surely Nature could hardly provide a more splendid spectacle?

But – what was this? From out of the white-fanged jaws of this nautical monster there spat one – two – three – more, six – seven, perhaps a dozen – puny human beings. One moment, it seemed, they did not exist: the next, like birds on wing, they zoomed forward on the very crest of the huge waves and were shot at extraordinary speed along the surface of sea-washed sand.

Mr Pemberton had never seen anything quite so remarkable in all his life. To say that he was fascinated would be inadequate. He was mesmerised, hypnotised; he stood where he was, as if chained to the spot. In vain did his friends attempt to persuade him to continue with their stroll: their words were not only disregarded, they were not even heard. 'I'll see you later on,' muttered Mr Pemberton vaguely. But in some way, already, he was casting off anchor.

After a while Mr Pemberton climbed over the parapet and walked across the soft sands to be able to watch more closely the activities of the scattered group of surfers. He watched in open-mouthed admiration as these gladiators, arming themselves with no more than the flimsiest length of curved board, strode forth to do battle with the mighty sea. Even before they entered the water they looked puny and pitiful, and once they were surrounded by clouds of froth and surf, their minute helplessness seemed emphasised. Yet it was these same small heroes who, moments later, came hurtling on the sea's back with all the natural pride of true victors.

Mr Pemberton was not only amazed, not only intrigued – he was captivated. He walked up and down at the edge of the sea almost wanting to cheer the surfers on. Jolly well done, sir, he thought, as one very daring swimmer shot down a veritable mountain of a wave. Oh, good show, good show – as another figure executed an almost perfect landing at high speed. Oh – well done, well done, well done ...!

It was then that the aforesaid tiny voice began to whisper in Mr Pemberton's ear those fatal words: *why not have a go yourself?* Why ... not ... yes, why not ... indeed? The more Mr Pemberton listened to the little voice (it was louder now) the more the idea called to him, like some clarion rallying call. After all – he watched a man old enough to be his father float effortlessly upon the bosom of an enormous wave – there was no real reason why he shouldn't. He was on holiday, wasn't he? And he had got a costume, it was back in the car, there. Well, hurry then, snapped the insidious voice, as if just a little tired of having to whip up enthusiasm for a patently good cause.

Mr Pemberton hurried, he even ran most of the way back to the car. When he got there he found, to his consternation, that his friends were preparing to leave. This was perhaps a preliminary moment of truth: he did not waste time trying to persuade them to stay, he hastily removed his suitcase and murmured reassuringly that he would be all right, but he'd stay on here for a while, and see them back in town. Then, to the accompaniment of their concerted, astonished stare, Mr Pemberton turned and hurried back to those waves which, instinct told him already, would not wait for ever.

At the end of the parapet Mr Pemberton found a small hut where surf boards were offered at 1/- an hour, deposit 5/-. Seizing the first that came to hand he plunged on down over the sands, seeking a suitable spot wherein to divest himself of encumbering clothes, and prepare for his great initiation.

Like all true-blue Englishmen Mr Pemberton clung to the belief that he could undress without exposing any important part of his body, a superhuman task involving matador-like manoeuvres with a small towel. However, at last the feat was accomplished, and Mr Pemberton — all white six feet of him — set course for the sea, clutching to his breast the long tapering surf-board.

It is perhaps some indication of Mr Pemberton's determined character that he was prepared to embark on surfing without any more experience than having watched, in some awe, those more professionally skilled than he. True, as he waded purposefully out into the shallow waters he kept a weather eye open on surfers around him: he noted that they tucked the base of the board into the pit of their stomachs, and that their outstretched hands held the top curve of the board at either side ... But then spectators at cricket matches can watch how Test batsmen execute their graceful and glorious strokes ...

When Mr Pemberton was in about three feet of water he turned, as he had seen the other surfers do, and waited. He was not, to tell the truth, quite sure what he was waiting for; but on the reasonable assumption that it was the next wave he glanced quickly at the approaching white wall, and obeying a blind wild impulse, most mistakenly, launched himself forward as he had seen so many other surfers do.

It must be admitted that the next few turbulent moments had a disturbing effect on Mr Pemberton's initial morale. Far from soaring forward gracefully, he was brutally knocked sideways, his surf-board was torn from his grasp, and before landing spreadeagled on the wet sands he turned two or possibly more somersaults. A lesser mortal might have retired there and then, but after getting back his wind Mr Pemberton gritted his teeth, retrieved his surf-board which was floating away rapidly, and plunged back into the fray, or rather surf.

Surf, Mr Pemberton now discovered, was a term synonymous of many things: a cloud of innocent spray, or a vast mountain of solid water — a froth of gentle rain or a thunderous downpour of Atlantic venom — it was all, technically, surf. The only trouble was that Mr Pemberton seemed unable to ride it. Indeed the simile was not inapt, for the sea seemed to have turned into a bucking broncho determined to unseat Mr Pemberton at every forlorn attempt to sit in the saddle. No matter how he tucked his surf-board in, no matter how fierce his grip, how pronounced his waiting crouch – whether he threw himself before or after or even during a wave – none of it seemed to make any difference. The result was depressingly the same, a cascade of drenching water, a forlorn tug of war with the surf-board, several loud splashes and gurgles and screams from Mr Pemberton – and the final ignominious delivery of his bruised and battered body on the bare sands.

How long this suffering might have been endured, who knows? – Mr Pemberton was doggedly determined to master his new craft no matter at what cost. But suddenly as he waded mournfully out again to meet yet another onslaught, it seemed as if some bright-eyed mermaid, some green-eyed wonder of the deep was sent to his aid. 'You are a silly boy,' she said in honeyed tones, 'You're doing it all wrong. Now look, just you watch me. Here's a wave coming, now one – two – three – go!'

As the wave boomed and broke all around him Mr Pemberton struggled to keep his feet, and looking around to see nothing but flying surf, decided the mermaid must indeed be a creature of his imagination. But no – as the spray cleared, he could just dimly see the dark crown of her head as she reached, triumphantly, the distant shore.

A few minutes later she was back at his side, whispering encouragement. 'Go on with you now, I was just as bad when I started. You just need confidence. Now why don't you come with me this time? Here we go then – watch out – one – two – three – and GO!'

This time – this time, too, Mr Pemberton went. He went with the mermaid, with his surf-board – above all with the wave. It was as if he was caught up magically and marvellously, at least for a moment, by something altogether outside his previous experience. It was terrifying, of course, quite terrifying; at one moment Mr Pemberton seemed to be poised high in space, like a bird – at the next, whoosh – and he was soaring, ah, yes at last soaring, down and down and down

– terrifying, yes, but oh how wonderful, how marvellous, how exhilarating!

Words failed Mr Pemberton, as slowly he returned to this earth, while his surf-board planed gently to a stop at the tip of the wave-ridden beach. For a while he could only mutter and grunt, half with shock, half with pleasure.

'Hey, there,' called out that same honeyed voice. 'Once isn't good enough – you've got to do it again and again and again ...'

Turning with a sheepish smile, and gathering himself once more for the fray (though this time more confidently) Mr Pemberton saw, it seemed to him for the first time, that his mermaid was a fairly realistic image of a brown and healthy, and rather pretty young girl in a swim suit. Her name, it later transpired, was Pam.

But none of this really mattered at the moment. All that mattered was to get back into the water, to wade through those first shallow waves, to venture further and further until the mountains rose around you, and then at last – like the matador with his bull – to seek that moment of truth, that instinctive time of knowing – *Now!* – and to launch yourself, like an eagle into flight, upon the incoming wave.

It would be untrue to say that Mr Pemberton spent every remaining moment of his holiday surfing. There was a need to eat and sleep, and also to improve upon this miraculous meeting with a mermaid called Pam who turned out, conveniently, also to come from London. And yet surfing was the peak, the ultimate – in surfing Mr Pemberton suddenly understood himself, was released, consumed, and returned to himself a gayer, more exhilarated, more exciting person than before. There were moments, as he caught a particularly high wave and came riding in at a speed which if not greater than light he felt sure was ahead of sound, when he knew he was with the gods themselves. Somehow he knew, and if he didn't that little voice, rather bolder now, would have told him, that after all this, a dull life in the city would never be enough ... which in the event proved exactly so, although fortunately by then he had the added permanent advantage of a mermaid's company.

So perhaps next time you go surfing you had better be very careful ... and then again, perhaps not.

VI

A Man and a Trumpet

The trumpet lay across the dark background of Tucker's lap, its bright shape half hidden by his thick, stubby fingers, by the spreading flesh of flabby hands. When the trumpet was like that it became what for some people it would always be, a metallic inanimate object, a compound of brass and silver, not even graceful to the eye. There was no apparent purpose to it, no link between it and the hands. Even Tucker seemed to feel this. While the hands wrapped awkwardly around the trumpet, the rest of his body, standardised in the same dull evening dress as the other members of the band, slouched in a shapeless position of unrest; as though to demonstrate a dissatisfaction with the trumpet, as with many other things.

Around Tucker the other players exchanged remarks, smoked cigarettes, glanced idly through the piled sheets of music. In one way or another their presence was established, their behaviour related to that of their environment: the big glass-domed dance hall, the fuzzy mist of stale-smelling smoke, the rising and falling chatter of waiting dancers squatting around scattered tables, bunching in groups at the entrances.

Tucker, however, gave no impression of being related to any part of the dance hall, least of all to the yellow trumpet. He was a big lanky figure, shoulders hunched up, long legs crossed, a square head only lightly covered with thinning ginger hair. Around his mouth a colony of tiny flexible muscles had grown, and from time to time these twitched and fluttered. When this happened the movement translated itself to the eyes and for a moment they might widen with slight surprise, revealing their light greyness. Otherwise the eyes remained almost closed against the smoke, looking away, out of contact and interest with anything immediate. A casual onlooker would have seen the trumpet, the sprawled figure, the well-thumbed wads of music, the square gold-and-crimson tapestry stitched across with the name of the band; each item as apparently lifeless as the other.

But when the lights dimmed and Doyle, the band-leader, gave his signal, scattering an opening chord across the piano-keys, the transition was a pronounced one. As though by some subtle pre-arrangement the shaded rose-coloured spotlight glanced against the trumpet, lighting up its curving frame.

When Tucker raised the trumpet to his lips the movement created a winking and gleaming, a spinning round of light, so that watching eyes were hypnotised towards the trumpet alone. There was suddenly nothing disjointed, only a gentle flow about everything, beginning with Tucker, no longer sprawling but standing firm and leaning slightly forward, like a tree with the wind – ending with the slow outstretch of his arms reaching to the culminating spotlighted apex. The trumpet, alive, took a bold lead of the other instruments and brought a quickening of movement to every pair of legs, stirring them, even in the pall-smoke of a hot, twentieth-century dance hall, with faint memories of ancient tribes and rituals. Some dancers were seized up by the trumpet music and whirled round more wildly than before; others were sung into silence and cessation, so that they stood listening and worshipping.

Many of the tunes were hardly tunes at all, or distortions of olden tunes, but somehow the trumpet gave to them a new life. When the trumpet fell silent, something strange and wonderful was lost. In the bright light there was a man in a chair holding a piece of dead silver metal; the smoke grew thicker, the chatter chattered into banalities, and the dancers and Tucker were both missing something though neither of them quite knew what it was or quite that they missed it.

Tucker had had the trumpet a long time. It was only the second one he had ever owned. The first he had bought on the hire purchase, when he was seventeen. It took him three years to pay off, and by that time the trumpet, in doubtful condition when he got it, was past worth repairing. But it had served its purpose: he could play, and play well, could play sweet haunting dance music, or swing, or creditable scraps of the classics – or, as he liked most of all, the strange, wandering blues versions of old negro spirituals. When he finally bought a new trumpet he chose carefully. He had taken it everywhere with him since; a matter of ten years. He had the same case, too, a strong, black leather case with a brass lock. The trumpet fitted neatly into the satin-cushioned compartment and the lid folded over and clicked, shutting it up in a world of its own. Tucker seldom, if ever, allowed the case to stray from his gaze and his watch on it was lover-like. Yes, lover-like, because even after ten years he could only say that he knew the trumpet as well as lover knows lover: that is, there was always something finally unpredictable. He could never say, like the mathematician or the rationalist, tonight I will perform in such and such a manner, according to this or that pattern. He could only perform.

He spent much of his time groaning with exasperation at the trumpet's demands, wondering at the persistence of his confirmation to the one way of life. He knew there were many trumpeters as good and better, technically, than himself. He could never play strictly by the book, with all the will in the world. But the improvisation, the exultant self-creations, had a queer face-saving way of matching the ordained music. Because of these things he got by, was forgiven, was tolerated – was even admired by other players. Within himself he remained unsure and unsatisfied: he could never quite understand why he should spend his life blowing a trumpet, night by night, band by band, place by place.

Looking back, that life, ten years of it, was a helter-skelter of one-night sessions, Sunday concerts, smoky cafés and steady drum beats; the raucous laughter of London music halls, the polite applause of suburban cinemas, the dreary trail round belching provincial cities and second-rate holiday towns. Ultimately there came the flat champagne atmosphere of night clubs – among them he could have stayed, drawing fat cheques, rooting himself into the world of high society and fantasy living. But he was restless and unfulfilled. In the summer he joined a competent self-contained sextet, came with them down to this red-bricked holiday resort tucked along the coast. The hours were long, the work arduous; but there were sunshine days, a sea lapping almost at the doorstep, fine golden sands along which he could walk for miles every morning, sniffing the sea-weed scented air and blowing away the taint of smoky dances. To the dance hall (no better and no worse than most) he came and played and went away and came back and played and went away again; and the days went leisurely by. Only at the back of his mind was there a slight worrying sense of incompletion. Of the solution he could not be sure, save that perhaps it had something to do with a trumpet, yellow-silver in the dancing light. Or perhaps not.

In the afternoons, through the gentle drift of *thé dansants*, the band took things easily. There were talkative family parties filling the tables, in for the day from more outlying villages; school children, quite a few tired infants from the beach, young couples in university blazers and tennis shirts. It was a leisurely time, spoons clinking in saucers, steaming teapots, plates of fruit cakes, neat bowls of cream and strawberry jam. Visitors came in everyday clothes, the waitresses wore light blue, summery afternoon costumes. There was no smart, smiling white-fronted master of ceremonies – in fact, no MC at all, only an unimpressive assistant. Even the daylight, sinking in opaquely through the wide dome, added to a curious impression of absent glamour. It was merely a crowd of holidaymakers transferred from sitting along the promenade into the slightly greater privacy of the dance hall. There was no glitter, no tawny tints, no air of fantasy, as there might be in a night world of artificial light. Everything was subdued, and the music must fit the mood. They played soft, easy tunes, slow fox-trots, many sweet waltzes – with Doyle's hands wandering sleepily about the piano and the drummer half dozing as he maintained the ponderous rhythmic background. The two saxophones and clarinet, Tucker's casual muted notes, ebbed and flowed appropriately. Couples took the floor and danced competently. Much more important was talking over the teapot, the afternoon gossip, cocked ears, blobs of jam spread generously over the bread — another cup of tea and the knowledge of sunshine outside.

At night it was a different world. Tucker came in about eight o'clock from a stroll along the beach. His nostrils quivered at once, smelling the familiar stale atmosphere, partly created by the dancers, partly a content of the very hall itself. It was hot, to be hotter; dry, to be nearly dried up; tasting sour on the mouth so that he usually drank several pints of beer every evening. Yet the very familiarity had a curious attraction, drawing him towards it despite himself. Away, sitting in the bedroom of his boarding-house or taking a bus-ride out of the town, he would think with horror of coming back and burrowing into the sticky hotness, playing through the score or two of tunes, known so well.

Yet when he arrived he found a pleasure, even an excitement, out of embarking on the ritual — walking across the shiny dance-floor, exchanging a greeting with the others, sorting out the music, opening the case, fingering the trumpet, adjusting his cushion, blowing a few off-key notes; putting down the trumpet, taking a slow pensive breath. The sense of purpose, of direction, fascinated even as it repelled. He waited impatiently for the moment when he could raise up the trumpet and blow it to life again ...

The people streaming in were not those of the *thé dansant*; those would not have fitted so easily into this half-ghost world. Here was, mostly, the high flush of youth, bright brittle colours striking jagged, unorthodox pathways. Tucker looked unemotionally at the women in their glittering dance frocks, some in gold and shimmering silver, others in white taffetas with low backs, and some black laced, with cool nets and soft sprays of flowers. A few, by contrast, still wore puffed-out afternoon dresses, blue-green like the sea. The dresses, bunched together, patterned into brilliant rainbows, colour upon colour; the faces were less defined, more uniform in their half-lifted smiles, the shake of fluffy hair, the momentary excitement of white throats. The pattern formed and reformed, grouping near to the bandstand and sometimes hushing in expectancy. At last Doyle rubbed a handkerchief between fat, sticky hands, dropped it carelessly, and tapped three times with his toe ... The men in the band were glad to break out of the waiting silence. They always, though later losing brilliance through weariness, swung into the opening tunes with a daring, natural unison.

One night, like this, Tucker became aware that he was being watched. There might be three hundred pairs of eyes looking towards the band, but seldom more than a dozen really watched: when someone watched you, a particular player, it could be felt out of all the haze and noise and shuffling movements. They were all, Tucker was, used to the group of adoring fans, clustering around the footlights. But this was different. It was not the open, evident worship from a few feet away. Tucker first felt it, from quite a long way, when he was in the middle of a slow blues passage. If he had stopped to think why or where he would have lost himself, the band, the tune. He closed his eyes and pushed out the notes, his lips sinking deeper into the mouthpiece, remaining aware, no more, of the watching. As the passage ended they gave him a clap, a genuine clap, more than politeness, a thing that could always please him. He smiled vaguely and peered about in the smoke, fancying he heard one clap of hands above others: but to the eye all hand-clapping looks alike.

The next time it was his solo he knew again that he was being watched, and he managed to flick a quick glance round, between a break of bars. It took him more time than that, but later in the evening his eyes reached their destination; he saw the girl in the cream-white dress with a crimson bow. She was sitting alone at a small table at the far end of the hall, her elbows propped on the table and her face resting between cupped hands. Her hair was blonde, rather faded, coiled in a bunch at the back. Through the haze of smoke the girl appeared to Tucker as something not quite definable. Whether because of the creamy dress he could not be sure, but he had the impression of something light, even fragile – of something wisp-like that might drift away with the wind – as he looked across and met, alight in the centre of the pale, oval face, the frankly staring eyes.

The eyes did not turn away. He had a feeling that they had not directly noticed his own recognition, as though fixed on him they were seeing through and beyond. Curiosity grew upon him, and for the remainder of the evening he studied the girl carefully. He noted that she was alone, that every now and then someone came and asked her for a dance, but no particular one – a soldier, a sailor, a suave middle-aged business man, a young college lout. When she threaded among the tables to the dance-floor – not now looking towards him – he saw that she was even more delicately shaped than he had imagined. She was not particularly young, yet there was a curious transparency about her, most of all about her face and neck, that conveyed an impression of the flame of youth, burning up. When she danced she seemed to float over the ground, as if so light as almost to ride on the air. Watching, covertly, he detected some paradox about the girl's appearance. There was a false brightness: her face – white, with a bright red flicker in the cheeks – reminded him of a doll's face. Even her dress, frothing to an abrupt end, exposing the slow, thin curve of her legs, did not seem a natural part of her. He felt he could have imagined her against a cool, limpid background, soft shadows and the beauty of reflected water – a creature of leisurely, flowing time. But here there was an impatient, almost a gaudy façade that he could not understand.

The girl was there the next evening. The band opened with 'Stardust', their signature. The saxes soared into the first swell of music, then Tucker broke in with his sweet, gentle transcription of the melody. He held the trumpet downwards, his head shaking backwards and forwards. Looking along the thin golden stem of the trumpet his eyes found, across the dance floor, the same table. At first he could not be completely sure it was occupied – as if half of his seeing was turned inwards, upon the playing of the tune, and what he saw beyond lay in a region of transparency. He blinked once, and again, and as he held on to the last dying note his eyes cleared and then he was sure that at the same table was the same girl. She was staring, again. He turned the trumpet-head in her direction and blew the last notes with a sudden inflection. The girl's eyes brightened momentarily; then, as the tune ended, she turned away. Tucker watched the swift curve of her side-face, her forehead, her neck. It struck him, oddly, that they were as white as the table-cloth.

This time the girl did not often dance. He was sorry and wondered why not. On the few occasions she was on the floor he watched her with greater attention. The rest of the time the distance was sufficient to emphasise the impression of transparency, as if there might so easily be no one there at all. Watching her he became aware of a certain sense of detachment. It was something like he felt about playing his part in the band, about fulfilling his contribution, awaiting the coming solo. A feeling of inevitability about which you were curious, but passively curious – not actively, not inquisitively curious. There was a time coming and something you were going to do or experience; if you sat and worked it all out like arithmetic with your mind you would never do and never know; you just had to wait, unworrying, and when the time came the thing existed or it did not, the music you played was you and alive, or it was nothing and it was dead. That was the way he felt about the girl, about her being there, and why, and what it meant.

He met her the next morning, watching the Punch-and-Judy show near the pier pavilion. She was standing with feet astride, lips wide-parted and a sudden dance of laughter in her eyes. Like a child, he thought, like a child with painted white cheeks. He met her without pre-meditation. He found himself standing beside her and that he was laughing as she was laughing, and as a hundred sticky-faced children were laughing. At the end of the laugh they turned at the same time and laughed at each other. Then she stopped laughing and looked, he thought, a little sad, a little regretful. 'Hullo?' he said, curiously.

They walked along the promenade, a wide curving promenade that almost encircled the sea, with two gaunt peninsula heads rising up at either end. The girl hardly came up to his shoulders. She walked rather slowly, with careful footsteps. She wore no hat and her short blonde hair fluffed up in the wind, making her head seem big and out of proportion to the rest of her body – a bright flower swaying on a slender stem. They did not talk a great deal, nor did they refer pointedly to the dance hall, the trumpet, or the watching. Tucker talked in a high-pitched unfamiliar voice, he did not know why. The girl's voice was low, almost a whisper, so that he could not trace its origin, whether she was from north or south, east or west. He could only guess that she came from a world of cities, perhaps a brittle, hard world. But she, he learned, was not so.

They walked out along the pier, to where the anglers fished, slow patient men with all day to spare. An elderly black-coated trio was playing chamber music in the open air concert theatre: it and the sombre, rather sleepy audience seemed out of place at the tip of the pier, where the land began to seem less important, where you could look down between the cracks in the boards and see the green of the sea. At the end of the pier they felt the tug of the sea wind. Tucker noticed it brought a soft glow of red to the girl's cheeks; but also that she looked tired. They walked back more slowly. On the way he stopped at one of the little kiosks, insisting that they both posed for an elderly gentleman terming himself the Professor, who created black and white silhouettes of them within three minutes for half a crown. They exchanged their black profiles and walked on, a little shy of each other. Soon she left him, hearing the boarding-house lunch-gongs ringing out along the front. He watched her disappear – a small, lonely figure – into a friendless hotel.

He saw her every morning after that. It was all rather unreal, as though part of a dream. Without any pre-arrangement they would somehow find each other watching the Punch-and-Judy show. Afterwards they would stroll about – or, since the girl often seemed tired, they would sit on one of the long benches running along the promenade walk, watching the couples strolling backwards and forwards. It was soothing to sit there and let the sunlight pour into you; gradually relaxing, not often talking; just sitting in harmony and letting the morning drift by. And at night the girl came to the dance hall, always sitting at the same table, always alone. Now he smiled openly at her, in the interval he went and sat at the table; once he danced with her, finding her loose and unweighted in his arms. But ultimately, he realised, his real meaning for her existed when he played the trumpet. And so he was glad to be playing. When he played he did so for her, seeking to express something which he could not express in words, nor even fully understand.

Towards the end of the week he had his free afternoon. He met the girl after lunch. They took a bus to the far end of the town and set out along the stubby head-land. It was a brilliant day, the sun drying the grass into cracked, yellow partitions under their feet. Tucker walked with new vigour, feeling once again the unspoiled wind coming across the bay. Beside him the girl wore a cool, flimsy, maroon-blue summer dress. Creasing up with the wind it emphasised, shadowily, the small, thin flow of the girl's body. He thought how easy it would be to pick her up, light like a leaf, and to launch her gently into the arms of the wind to be swept away – just like a leaf. A feeling of tenderness came upon him. He wanted very much to put his large, stronger arms around the girl, to give her some sort of support or protection. But he guessed it was not to be done.

He found himself talking more naturally. He had no aroused emotions towards the girl; he felt no idle sentiment, no wild passion; he knew he was not in love with her or she with him. He saw her as nothing beautiful, though possessed of a certain wistful prettiness. Yet, looking sideways, he felt a sudden warmth, as of understanding, and he loosened his own tautness and began talking and laughing, telling her about all the years of the trumpet; the years behind and the years ahead, the long wandering journeys, the wonders and the heartaches of it all. He said, in momentary anger, I ought to throw away the so-and-so trumpet, go and do something really worthwhile. What a life standing on a bandstand and blowing into a horn, eh? he half-asked, again. But the girl merely laid a hand lightly on his arm and shook her head. He could hardly feel the arm's weight but he felt a warmth, as of sudden wisdom and assurance, that he would always remember.

He talked at length, probably too much. Sometimes he pulled himself up, apologetically, but the girl always motioned him to go on. Occasionally she nodded or smiled some appreciation. Whenever he asked her anything she hesitated and answered slowly; a few words at the most. She spoke very quietly so that often he had to bend forward to catch what she said. She spoke almost in a whisper. It should, perhaps, have seemed odd, but with her it seemed to belong, it was all part of the curious impression of transparency and intangibility.

It did not take them long to reach the head-land. It was a wide sand-bunkered place, popular with holidaymakers from the town. Here and there the groups were spread out, sunning themselves and having teas. But further, where the grass ended in a sea of sand, there was more solitude. They went along slowly, savouring the freedom of escape.

'How far out would the sea be?' asked the girl suddenly. There was the faintest touch of breathlessness in her voice. Tucker wondered whether he guessed correctly in thinking she was flushed with excitement – 'Oh! I'm glad I've been here, once, anyway,' the girl went on – and he guessed his guess was correct.

'I don't rightly know,' he said, shading his eyes. The tide seemed to be lost over the horizon.

'There it is!' he cried, pointing to the wink of a crooked white line. Coming in, he judged; and they went to greet it.

They stopped just out of reach of the creeping water, watching the leading waves urging onward and onward, each time devouring a particle more, a mound more, a world more of sand. There was about the advance something inexorable and final – yet also, it seemed to Tucker's fascinated gaze, a certain grandiose beauty.

To his surprise the girl shivered, though the sun was as hot as ever.

'Like the fingers of a clock,' she whispered, puzzlingly. And she turned and began walking away without looking back.

They walked steadily, for a long time in silence. Once again he felt that she was tired. Now and then he deliberately called a halt, ostensibly to examine a coloured stone or a stranded jellyfish, and he sensed her gratitude. As they approached the grass slopes he looked at her curiously.

'Have you enjoyed it?' he said.

She smiled.

'Oh, yes ... So much.'

He went on, uncertainly.

'You mentioned earlier about being glad you've been once anyway – won't you come again?'

The girl's teeth suddenly pressed tight together, almost as in physical agony.

'No,' she said, and the word hissed out hot with a bitterness that was beyond his understanding.

'Because,' – she said later, when they were sitting in the bus and watching the view from the headland disappearing behind a curve in the road – 'you see, I go back on Sunday.'

And though he could understand a certain sadness at the approaching end of a holiday, why, it seemed to him that the way she spoke it was the end of a world. Indeed, as he left her he knew there were tears, and for a whole ending world, in her eyes.

She was sitting in the usual place in the evening. It was outwardly the same as other evenings: the steady, recurring sequence of tunes – slow fox-trot, quick-step, waltz, rumba, slow-fast-slow-fast-slow-fast – the growing hilarity of the holiday parties, the inevitable sozzled young man attempting to climb up on the bandstand. And yet he felt that for him it was not even the same as the previous evening, but that upon him there was yet a further demand. He wondered about it –

in the intervals between playing, fingering idly at the neat button-keys of the trumpet, rubbing the ball of his first finger round and round and round, as if polishing – was still wondering each time Doyle caught his eye with an inclination of his shiny bald head, so that, slowly and obediently, he brought the mouth-piece over his lips.

When at last he broke into his brassy song he gave to it a new power, almost an urgency, and the melodies seemed to possess an unexpected purity and innocence. Once or twice the crowd gave him a spontaneous applause, that was insistent for encores. When Doyle looked at him inquiringly, podgy hands poised over the piano, he nodded and without hesitation slid the name of the tunes out of the corner of his lips. He did not think about them; the names seemed to be there ready, and somehow he felt they were always the sort of tunes that meant something to the girl. Mostly they were the old favourite tunes, the ones you could do almost anything with on a trumpet, like 'Margy' and 'Basin Street' and 'Honeysuckle Rose' and 'St Louis'. They could be played fast or medium, or standing on their head for that matter. They caught up a listener and set his feet tapping and his heart singing. The way Tucker played them, his face tight and a little grey with the concentration, they had an enormous sense of slow, majestic movement, needing no more in the world than the subdued heart-beat of the drummer, the faintest of sad echoes high pitched on the piano. The message of the trumpet was a calling one, trembling through the body, stirring the laziest couples in the hall into movement. It brought the girl to her feet, too. She came, swaying slightly, her cheeks puffed out by a singing tongue, and she danced once, twice, even three times. But after that she danced no more in the whole evening: after that she looked tired, was a transparent ghost, already seeming to belong to a transparent world of her own.

He saw her for the last time on the Saturday night. She looked pale and suddenly shrunken. He wondered if she had been crying. She sat at the usual table, watched him as usual; but there was something lacking. He saw her order drinks, tilt the glasses up without interest. Once or twice she coughed and her shoulders shook wearily. He felt as if she were struggling to go through the performance of a play. In the middle of one tune he was disturbed to see that she was getting ready to go. He watched out of the corners of his eyes, busking the phrases while his mind raced over to her. Something tempted him to stand up and call out, above the wailing music and the murmuring voices: No! Don't go! – there's something I don't understand. He felt, though without any real belief, that there must be something else he could do for her.

She got up quietly from the table and walked to the door. He saw her turn and look towards him. He was hot from playing and little driblets of sweat dripped down his forehead, clouding his eyes. Her face danced at him through a white mist. He blinked, smiled for a moment with cracking lips, letting the trumpet die off. He knew she must have smiled back. But she had gone.

When the tune was finished he slipped over to the table. He had a wild idea that perhaps she had left something, some sort of message or explanation. But the table was bare, yielding nothing to the swift feel of his searching hands. As a last hope he pulled back the chair. Crumpled up in the centre was a tiny handkerchief; hers. She had left something then! He felt instinctively that it was meant for him, as a symbol, a secret memento. The handkerchief looked small and lonely, as she had first seemed to him. He picked it up gently and put it in his pocket.

When he was back on the bandstand he pulled it out again, aware of slight uneasiness. He supposed in a way a person's whole character might easily be understood from a tiny speck, from a tiny crumpled handkerchief. He opened out the handkerchief carefully, in a gentle, rather sad movement: it was stained with bright red patches of blood. Why, he thought, there's blood on the handkerchief, and her shoulders shook every time she coughed; that's why there's blood on the handkerchief ...

And then Doyle's face slanted towards him and Doyle's

white beckoning hand rose and fell through the air like the slap of a bird's wing. He felt the sudden throb of life of the drums and the sudden wail of life of the saxes and the shrill trill of life of the clarinet, and automatically his two hands picked up the trumpet and raised it high in the air. On the very last of the down beats Tucker came in, on a long harsh note, holding it for a daring split-second longer than the text-books would allow – and then the trumpet was away on its own, telling the story, painting the melody in a brassy twilight. It was Tucker playing, the voice a living voice, blaring out with an anguished echo as it created anew the slow dirge of a heartaching Harlem blues, born three thousand far miles away. Tucker, all of him, creating a voice and a music; the face suddenly softened and the eyes closed, the frowns falling away and the long bones catching the glare from electric lights and seeming to be supernaturally illuminated ... Or perhaps not quite all of him, for there was a small part not there but wandering out of the hall and far away, searching for a small, lonely figure that had disappeared into the world's great darkness. As the figure went along the shoulders hunched up and shook and coughed away life and everything else hunched up and shook and coughed away life until the movement came wave upon wave, until there was a vast transparent sea, until even the transparency was fading and disappearing, until there was no sound but an echo, whispering 'Like the fingers of time' – until even the echo ebbed and flowed and faded away, like the waves of an outgoing tide.

Tucker went on playing, the tune seeming like it would never end, and nobody minding. There was the drums and the saxes and Doyle bunched tight over the piano, and the dancers crowding round like the sea round the rocks – only they were standing and staring, not swallowing up, like the sea. Tucker played the chorus over and over and over, not because it was anybody's particular chorus but just because it was what he was playing at that time. The way Tucker played that night it sounded like something that had never been heard before and perhaps would never be heard again. Everyone who heard could have told that something had happened to a man, and that man was Tucker. The thing that had happened comes to most of us one day or another, but the fact is it can never be explained in words. In the case of Tucker it was something to do with a yellow trumpet and the noise it made, a man blowing himself into it and how that could *mean* to just someone else in this great living-and-dying world of ours.

VII

A Literary Letter

My Dear Young Friend:

It is very kind of you to write in admiration of my work, and so astutely to analyse the influence upon it of the late lamented Marsden Bennetts. Therein, if you will pardon a digression, lies a short story. My own admiration for the writings of Marsden Bennetts was of even longer standing than my marriage, but when the latter even took place it seemed only natural to try and communicate some of my enthusiasm to my new partner in life. Indeed, so fanatical was my devotion to the work of the man whom I regarded as something of a literary mentor that if my wife had happened to take a violent dislike to his opinions I believe, yes I really do believe that our very relationship might have been threatened. Fortunately Jane quickly came to share my own feelings: together we read and re-read those marvellously lyrical early poems, those wonderfully penetrating *avant garde* novels, and finally the fascinating volumes of memoirs. It is difficult, in retrospect, to say which we admired most, the lucid, limpid style – the bold even daring imagination – or the impressively mature wisdom. No, I don't think one can put a finger on any one facet, it was just the whole man in his enormous achievement – for us, Marsden Bennetts represented a truly great example of the creative human spirit at work.

'Wouldn't it be marvellous,' said Jane wistfully one day, 'to meet him?'

Well, of course, when you are an up and coming younger writer whose style and ambitions are modelled so devotedly and humbly upon that of the acknowledged master – when you have indeed exchanged a certain amount of master-pupil correspondence (even if this appeared to consist mostly of 10-page letters of mine analysing Bennetts' latest new book, with a brief card in return: 'Thanks. Keep Writing. Yours, Marsden') – then it should not be too difficult to arrange some kind of physical contact.

Nor was it. I wrote and told Marsden Bennetts that he now had an even more ardent disciple than myself, namely my new young wife, and that we both of us longed for the opportunity of expressing our mutual admiration to his face. Not long afterwards there came back one of those scrawling postcards, half unintelligible as usual, but unmistakably bearing an invitation to visit the great man next week-end. He mentioned that he was opening a local Book Exhibition at a university town not far from his country home and invited us to join him at that ceremony.

When we finally reached the town-hall where the opening ceremony was to take place a large crowd had gathered and the speakers were already lined up on the platform. We both immediately recognised Marsden ... that leonine face, that vivid shock of white hair, those striking gestures. Why, even without speaking he somehow drew attention more than all the others. And when finally he did speak, surprisingly – for most writers are dull and inarticulate in public – his personality came across even more strongly. It wasn't so much what he said, though that was often pithy and witty, but the way he *communicated* – it was impossible not to be aware of the power, the potency, of the speaker. Here, you felt, was a man whose whole being was fully alive and evolving, whose application to any problem would be forceful, one hundred percent all-embracing. Just as now, concluding a speech about his own craft.

'No good expecting authors to conform, to keep time-tables, to be docile and obedient – like you other everyday ordinary human beings. Authors are not really human, you see. How can they be? Everything they do is opposite to ordinary human ways. They sit up into the early hours of the morning wrestling not with their consciences but with that damned blank white sheet of paper. The apex, the nadir of their achievement, is to cover that sheet of paper with lines of writing. Put like that it sounds rather banal, doesn't it? And yet – and yet – always remember – those lines of writing are new, unique, created – brought out of nowhere, fashioned for eternity ...'

There was much more like that, rambling, apparently uncoordinated chatter, yet seldom without point. When at last he sat down, the audience, though probably only half grasping what he had been saying, appreciated that they had been privileged to worship at the feet of greatness, and there was long and sustained applause.

After that came a tour of the exhibition and the signing of copies of his own books, while we hovered around humbly awaiting the right moment. When it came at last I hastily stepped forward and introduced myself.

'And this is my wife, Jane.'

At first it seemed almost as if Marsden Bennetts had completely forgotten about his invitation for he stared at me in utter blankness. But then as he saw Jane, looking I must admit rather radiant in the slinky new dress she had bought specially for the occasion, his face seemed to compose itself at once into alert awareness. Indeed, he seemed to bound to his feet, exuding a healthy animal liveliness.

'Why, *hullo*! So glad to meet at last.'

Momentarily his craggy hand held mine in his own, shaking it warmly ... but already, I noticed with some surprise, his whole attention seemed to be focussed not on his young literary devotee, but on the latter's wife.

'Aha, so *this* is your charming missus, eh? And where did you dig her up from, eh?'

Such jocularity, if rather unexpected, certainly helped to break the ice, and within a few minutes of meeting, all three of us were laughing and joking together as if we had known each other years. At close quarters there were several new features to be noticed about Marsden Bennetts. First, that outgoing personality that came over the footlights was no mischance, it really could be felt, almost as a physical impact. Second, though reputed to be nearly seventy, he really was confoundedly youthful looking; without prior knowledge I wouldn't have put him at much more than fifty. Thirdly – well, and I could see sharply that Jane was obviously reacting in the same way, the man was so damned attractive, there was no other word for it.

Attractive, I hasten to add, not in any obvious superficial way, but in his whole personality. There was no side, no pretence; ideas and opinions bubbled forth uninhibitedly and were all part of the resulting pattern; one just felt greatly drawn to the warmth and humour and well being.

'C'mmon,' said Marsden suddenly, when the tour of inspection was over. 'I'm tired of being literarily lionised – let's go and have a quiet drink.' He paused and winked at us in a delightful, confiding way. 'Just the three of us, eh?'

Well, of course, it was very flattering to be enfolded in this way into his secret circle, and so we tried to forget the tell-tale gnawing pains in our stomachs which reminded us that it was a long time since we had eaten, and followed Marsden out of the hall and round the corner to a snug little pub with oak beams and a real live ingle nook for which Marsden at once headed.

'Ladies first, of course,' he said with a gallant bow, and Jane was ushered into the corner, and Marsden then sat himself next to her, while I squeezed in on the outside. It was of course as it should be, I told myself, the lion in the centre, disciples either side. And yet somehow I couldn't help feeling there was something unsatisfactory about the arrangement. Every time I cleared my throat and endevoured to introduce some literary observation it seemed that Marsden's large white mane of hair was turned pointed away from me, and he was engaged in earnest conversation with Jane. Or rather, to be exact, he was talking and Jane was listening – the talk voluble and brilliant, the listening awed and concentrated. Once or twice, over the humped shoulder, I tried to catch Jane's eye, but somehow it proved quite impossible. Her own gaze seemed to be fixed almost implacably upon that no doubt expressive countenance, as if she was anxious to savour every moment of the great man's attention. Well, I thought to myself, I can hardly blame her. It was a rather special occasion. It was then, looking about me almost casually, that I happened to notice Marsden's left arm, lying casually along the top of the ingle nook. Almost imperceptibly it seemed to be dropping down and down ... and down ... until finally, with the simplest and most natural of gestures, it came to rest around the slim, youthful shoulders of his listener.

Of course, I told myself, it was just a natural gesture of human sympathy ... he had probably not noticed it even himself ... All the same I felt quite pleased when after a while Marsden suddenly broke off his peroration, looked at his watch and declared that perhaps we ought to be moving. Apart from anything else I had been reminded of the hollowness in my stomach, and I could see that Jane had this on her mind too. We were both probably looking forward to driving to Marsden's home and having something to eat.

Alas, this was not to be, for after travelling a mile or two in Marsden's noisy but rather exhilarating open sports car we pulled up at another country pub.

'Just one for the road, eh?'

I did not for one moment think of Marsden as a drunkard or tippler, even though during the next three hours we sampled the offerings of three further pubs ... no, it was obvious that he just enjoyed the stimulation of being out and about ... and of course talking, at least himself talking ... No doubt he found the company of a pretty young woman flattering, I thought rather sourly, sitting on a bench on my own at the latest pub while Marsden leaned against a wall, pinning Jane against it with one arm each side as he waxed eloquently to her about some trivial unliterary subject. Come to think of it, and naturally enough, Jane found his august attentions pretty flattering as well, I could see that by the brightness of her eyes and the pink flush of her cheeks. Ah well, I told myself, shrugging resignedly, one could really hardly complain.

So it came as quite a pleasant surprise when at last Marsden announced that we really were bound for home.

'Just a couple of miles further, then we turn off along a cart-track and there it is – pretty isolated you know really, but I love it. Gives me peace, absolute peace.'

'Ah, yes,' I said, sensing at last an opportunity to talk. 'That's how you work, isn't it, shut away from everyone.'

Marsden threw me a glance, almost the first, I fancy of the evening, and nodded.

'That is so. I have a hut at the bottom of the garden where I write.' He paused, and then said meaningfully, 'You must come and have a look at it.' But somehow he wasn't looking at me any longer, only at Jane, sitting beside him in the front of the car.

When at last we came to the drive leading to Marsden's house and turned off and began bumping along the lane it seemed to me that he fell suddenly into an uncomfortable silence – for a moment, almost, he exuded the aura of a worried man with a conscience.

'Is anything wrong?' I said at last.

'No, oh no, not really,' the great shoulders shrugged resignedly. 'I'm afraid we're a little late, that's all.'

This was about our only preparation for our entry into the brightly lit sitting room where, curled up half asleep in an armchair, we found waiting for us Mrs Marsden Bennetts. Somehow it had just not occurred to us that there might be a wife, above all a wife patiently waiting to receive guests whom, we gradually learned, she had been expecting since six o'clock.

'Never mind,' said Mrs Bennetts brightly, taking our coats. 'I've kept your suppers hot in the oven – I expect you're starving, aren't you?'

We were, of course, but rendered even more uncomfortably so by the realisation that dinner had been ready for the past four hours. And Marsden had never given a single indication of this surely significant fact! I could see, out of the corner of my eye, that Jane was finding this difficult to stomach – for there is one thing about Jane, she is a great believer in the equality of the sexes. Not so much in the obvious way, but from the point of view of consideration by one of the other. And Marsden's behaviour, trailing around from pub to pub, beguiling away the hours in the sunshine of a pretty girl's smiles and attention, while all the time he knew his wife had a meal in readiness at home, was curiously inconsiderate.

Moreover, at the end of what was a delicious, if rather overcooked meal, Jane ventured to say so. Marsden stared at her in astonishment.

'I beg your pardon?'

Jane repeated the accusation, while at the other end of the table, at which she had been largely ignored by her husband since sitting down, Mrs Bennetts fidgeted uncomfortably.

'Fiddlesticks!' said Marsden abruptly. 'Nonsense and fiddlesticks!'

I don't know who he thought he was talking to, perhaps he imagined he was still on some platform, but I wished I could have warned him in advance that a modern young woman, even a pretty one like Jane, can be quite a tarter if roused. However, by now embarked upon a great flow of inevitable rhetoric, Marsden was impossible to warn.

'... men are the creators, women are the sustainers. What great work of art has ever been created by a woman? None – none at all.' A sympathetic gesture here. 'Mark you, this is not to depreciate women. Women, as I say, are the sustainers, the nurturers ...' A gracious smile here across the table to a nervous Mrs Bennetts. '... Isn't that so, my dear? Why, I would be the first to agree that without my wife here, unobtrusively in the background, my work would be gravely affected ...'

He rambled on in this manner for some time while Mrs Bennetts fidgeted more and more and Jane went pinker and pinker trying to restrain herself. At last, rather like a time bomb too long delayed, she exploded – into a stream of scorching invective that would have done credit, I could not help thinking, to Marsden Bennetts himself. It was true that she belaboured mankind in general, but it could hardly be said that many of her remarks did not apply to Marsden in particular, and after a while he fell grimly silent.

At the end of it all he evaded Jane's still accusing glance and turned to me and said stiffly.

'Perhaps you would like to see my study?'

Uncomfortably I followed the tall white-haired figure out of the house and down across the wide lawn to the long hut standing in the corner. Once inside, though, I found myself falling under the spell again, as courteously but with a craftsman's pride Marsden showed me round his writer's den – pointing to the complex filing system, to the rows of original manuscripts, and finally to a bookcase stuffed full of editions of his books from all over the world – some, I remember, even printed in Japanese. Suddenly I felt humble again in the presence of such very real achievements ... I felt that British literature owed a great deal to a man of such high abilities.

While I was struggling to find the right words to express these feelings Marsden Bennetts took my arm in a friendly, but persuasive grip, and drew me towards him.

'I know you won't mind if I give you a piece of advice?'

'No, of course not.'

'Well, it's about your wife. Mmmmhh ... rather a headstrong young woman. I do think if I was you I would try and, er, keep her in check, eh?'

I can't remember what I said in reply, but it was something suitably non-committal. Later that night, when we lay rather restlessly in the bed in the spare room which Mrs Bennetts had carefully prepared for our comfort, Jane said primly:

'I suppose you know the old so-and-so made passes at me?'

'Well, I did notice in the pub ...'

'Huh! And what about *outside*, going to the car?'

I left the question unanswered, making its own rather sad commentary on the still night air. After all ...

'I still think he's a great writer.'

'Mmmh,' said my wife, and turned over and went to sleep.

In the morning we had breakfast with Mrs Bennetts – Marsden sent his apologies, she said, but he wasn't feeling very well. He remained incommunicado for the rest of the morning until the time had come for us to catch the once-a-day bus back into the nearby town. In fact it was little Mrs

Bennetts who came and waved us off: but I had little doubt that as soon as we had gone the white-haired old maestro would be bustling about and making his way down to that little hut in the garden, there to immerse himself in the less troublesome world of his imagination. And when I thought of him in that setting, indeed, I found a slight recovery in my estimation of him – which, I have to admit, had slipped somewhat in the course of our visit.

All of which my dear young friend, will perhaps help to explain why, regretfully, I must decline to encourage the proposed visit you and your no doubt charming and pretty young wife ...

VIII

Like Summertime

As long as I could remember I had set my heart on leaving the Cove. It would be a wrench parting from my mother, of course. My father had died when I was just a baby, drowned while out with the fishing fleet, and this had brought my mother and me much closer. My mother was like so many other Cornish women, a strong character with decided views of her own, an upright and respected person, devout attender at the local chapel and a righteous spirit if ever there was one. Yet to me she was always kind and loving, and I responded to her love without any sense of duty or pretence. Yes, I knew that I would be sad at parting from my mother.

But I did not feel any such regrets about the Cove, not at all. I admit it was a beautiful sight, the Cove, with the huge Atlantic waves swirling vengefully around the outer cliffs yet always thwarted by the sturdy harbour wall. I could see there was a quiet loveliness about the way the little grey cottage roofs rose in clusters, merging indefinitely into the larger area of granite-strewn moors behind them. Sometimes, too, I enjoyed leaning over the harbour wall and watching the long line of the fishing fleet bobbing up and down at anchor, like so many little painted dolls' boats.

But that was about all. For the rest the Cove, to me, represented a narrow, closed-in world that had perversely turned its back on all the excitement going on outside – the sort of world in which the state of health of Mrs Hosking, at the village stores, was apparently more important than the most vital international conference, where a lifeboat practice created more interest than any of the big events in London, and where the trivial debates of the parish council were followed more closely than any of those world-shattering goings on in the Houses of Parliament.

I don't quite know what bred in me this growing impatience. It was partly my mother's fault, perhaps, for encouraging me to read. I remember how when I was very young she always brought me back a pile of books from the travelling library, and then later on I used to attend, greedily, on my own account, bringing back bulky books with lurid covers – books of adventure stories, books about explorers, books about new discoveries. The world, I learned excitedly, was a huge and wonderful place, full of all kinds of astounding peoples and places, sights and experiences. Europe, Asia, Africa, America, whole continents lay awaiting my inspection. How could I possibly be expected to spend the rest of my life in the Cove?

I couldn't, and wouldn't; and in fairness to my mother I must say she never sought to oppose this wanderlust in me. Some of the other people in the Cove were less understanding, though, when I ventured to express my hopes and ambitions. At school, for instance, quite a few of the older boys looked on me as stuck-up and conceited, a 'big-head'.

I had my adherents, though. There was a little gang of us who used to spend most of the time together: the two Johns brothers, Willy and Dick, a boy called Peters who was the coastguard's son, Matthew Twigg from the farm up the hill, and young Karen Tregenza, whose father had the lobster-pot boat. I was the oldest of the group and so in the way of things became their leader. We used to wander up the cliffs looking for seagulls' eggs, and sometimes further afield, exploring the old ruined mine works out by Zennor. We were just like any other children's gang, I suppose, with our special rules and secret codes and pass-words, except that perhaps I brought in an extra touch of glamour with my extravagant promises of where I would lead them all one day. Sometimes when I got really warmed up to my theme the rest would sit down with open mouths drinking it all in like any adventure story.

Especially Karen. She was the youngest of the group, about thirteen at the time I first remember her, a small, dark girl, rather like an elf, with a short crop of raven black hair that fringed her round, serious face. She was the youngest of the group and I was the oldest so I suppose I acquired a feeling of responsibility towards her. We would climb the Treen rocks up to our secret summit where we sat with our legs dangling casually over the precipitous edge and always I would be impelled to look around to make sure that Karen was safely with us – and invariably I would find her watching me, her bright brown eyes alive with an obvious kind of hero-worship.

The others used to tease her about this, and then Karen would be upset, her puckish face twisting and her bright eyes misting suspiciously, and I would feel bound to protest. Once, indeed, Dicky Johns and I almost came to blows, both heated and flushed and glaring at one another – only halting when Karen gave a muffled cry and turned and ran away, weeping bitterly.

'Go on,' taunted Dicky, 'Look after your pet.'

Of course these seem childish tantrums now, but at the time they were very real emotions. I did feel bound to go after Karen and when I found her crouched on a boulder sobbing I put an uncertain hand on her shoulder.

'Don't cry, Karen. Please ...' I gave her a comforting squeeze. 'Here, I tell you what – let's go and have a look at the seagulls' nests. Maybe they've laid again.'

I suppose it was in this almost casual way that Karen and I began to go about together. We must have looked quite an odd pair at first, for as I say she was rather small at first, and I was on the tall side. But over the next year or two Karen suddenly seemed to blossom out, rather like one of those unfinished pictures to which the artist returns and quickly sketches in the remaining touches that make all the difference.

I noticed this vividly on the day I had arranged to take Karen into Penzance for the Corpus Christi Fair. We had to catch the six o'clock bus and I was waiting down on the wharf looking anxiously at the church clock, when suddenly a flicker of yellow caught my eye. I looked down the road and there was Karen coming towards me all dressed up to kill in a gay yellow taffeta dress with a white-ribboned straw hat perched prettily on her dainty head.

'Why, Karen,' I said involuntarily. 'You look – ' I was going to say something rather ordinary like 'lovely', but all at once the magic words came to my mind. 'You look like summertime!'

Karen blushed at the compliment and this merely emphasised her soft loveliness so that I felt suddenly very flattered to be taking her hand in mine and helping her on to the bus. And all the evening as we wandered up and down Market Jew Street looking in the brightly lit shop windows, and then afterwards walked towards the Recreation Ground that was already glowing with fairy lights and throbbing with the sound of hurdy-gurdies, I kept looking surreptitiously at Karen and thinking to myself – why, she's really pretty, like summertime, that's it, like summertime.

That evening, for the first time, I kissed Karen. It was when we were high up on the Big Wheel, dangling over the whole glittering universe, and I think it was a kind of exhilaration, a joy in being alive, that prompted me. But I fancy, on reflection, it was a much more meaningful event on her part ... and later that night when we had got off the bus and were walking back around our familiar little Cove I noticed Karen was strangely quiet.

'What's the matter?' I said at last.

She shook her head, under its unfamiliar covering.

'Didn't you enjoy yourself?'

She turned, and suddenly the words spurted out.

'Oh, yes, I did. It was wonderful, so wonderful. It was the happiest evening of my life. It was – '

She paused, as if too full of emotion to say more. Awkwardly I raised my hand.

'Here, take off that silly old hat and let's – '

But before I had done more than lift away the hat Karen had thrown herself into my arms with a curiously forlorn cry; and I, almost without thinking, was holding her tightly in our

first real embrace, murmuring in her ear.
'It's all right. Karen, it's all right ...'
It wasn't really, though, I suppose. After that, it's true, Karen and I were much closer. Our relationship was more clearly defined – we were 'walking out', as they would say in the Cove. But I know now – and if I am honest I suppose in some way I knew then – that our feelings weren't quite the same. I can only surmise at Karen's but I remember quite clearly what my own were. I was dominated more than ever by a single determination. Let the others do as they please, let Willy and Dicky take over their father's fishing boat, let Matthew work in the fields as his father had done and his father's father, let Roy Peters apply to join the coast-guards just like his father before him ... I was different. I was going to leave the Cove and go out into the big waiting world.

I used to talk about this sort of thing to Karen. Sometimes we would wander out towards Zennor over the moors, amidst the scent of heather and honeysuckle. There were soft patches of springy turf where you could throw yourself down and dream up at the summery blue sky.

Once I lay there with my head on Karen's lap and talked.

'You see, I don't want to be like all the others that just stay here and waste their lives. Even my mother's like that – her life begins and ends with the harbour walls. For her there isn't any other life, she doesn't want any other life ... But I do, I want space, freedom, opportunity ...'

I turned my head and looked piercingly up at Karen.

'You know what I mean? I've got lots of ideas. I'm pretty good at drawing, you know, and there are firms in London that will take you on and train you to be a draughtsman ... And then there's a lot of scope in commercial art, too – you know, advertising and all that sort of thing.'

I lay back and stared up at the sky again. It was a bright blue sky, coloured even brighter by the sun's reflected glare. It lay there before me like my future: a vast open sky of success, of future happiness.

'What do you think, Karen?' I said drowsily. 'Do you think I'll be a success?'

For quite a long time there was no sound, and then abruptly my blue sky was clouded over and I realised that Karen must have bent her head forward, and I felt her lips softly on my forehead.

'Yes, my darling,' she whispered. 'I'm sure you will, a great success. The world at your feet ...'

Yet I remember to this day not so much the kiss, but the single, salty tear that fell a moment later on my forehead and slowly trickled down until I felt the bitter taste on my tongue.

It wasn't very long after that when I left the Cove. At my mother's request the schoolmaster had made some inquiries up country and after some samples of my work had been sent to and fro it appeared there was a firm in the City of London who were prepared to take me on as an apprentice draughtsman. My mother was travelling up to London with me to make sure that I found respectable digs to live in and see me properly settled – after that it was up to me.

I can remember feeling nervous, but nothing more. This was what I had wanted for so long, it would have been hypocritical to have flinched. I was really quite excited when the morning came and my mother was bustling around as we waited for a taxi to take us to Penzance Station.

A little while before the taxi was due I went down the road and tapped on Karen's door to say goodbye. I was a little disconcerted to see that she had been crying, but I wasn't going to let this spoil the day's adventure.

'Come now, Karen,' I said. 'You know this is for the best, really. I mean – you do want to see me get on in the world, don't you?'

I hesitated, and then as she did not speak but just stood looking at me with a curious, sad sort of look – almost as if she was looking upon me for the last time, indeed. In the end I felt uncomfortable, and went on:

'Remember, I'll write to you every week, and you write too and give me all the news. And anyway, don't forget, it's only for a short while – I'll have a holiday at Easter, I'll be down then for sure.'

It was time for me to go. I looked quickly at Karen and her

blank eyes, suddenly filling with tears. I was about to remonstrate, to say something cheerful, when all at once I was swept by unfamiliar feelings of emotion, a constriction in my throat, a hint of pain ...

I raised my hand and touched Karen gently on her cheek, and then I smiled faintly.

'Don't worry, Karen, darling. I'll see you at Easter.'

But somehow I didn't. By the time that Easter came I had settled into my new life, working in my firm's big offices in the City and living in quiet humdrum digs out at Putney, and spending most of my spare time exploring all the wonders of a big city. It was all that I had imagined it, glitter and gloss, tinkle and tinsel, and something about all the brassy extravagance rather appealed to me. My work at drawing out engineering blue-prints, however, appealed to me rather less after a while. By now I had started attending evening classes at my local art school and there I met lots of students who had set their sights not on draughtsmen's offices, but on the more glamorous advertising agencies of Fleet Street and district. I began to haunt the Street in my spare time, studying the trade papers and applying for jobs – eventually I got taken on by one of the biggest agencies in the business. Something about my style evidently pleased them because in quick succession I had several different jobs and an equal number of rises. It was all hard, grinding work, often on overtime, but I found it exciting and, in a breezy, commercial sort of way, stimulating. There was little time to think about anything else, other than the immediate moment.

That was why, somehow, I never got around to returning to the Cove. I wrote diligently to Karen as promised, but somehow in the end they became letters of duty rather than of love. It was the distance, I told myself, but it was a distance much greater than that of the railway line from Penzance to London, I knew. Somehow when the taxi went up the hill from the harbour and the bend cut off my last view of the Cove I suppose I had determined at that moment to put it out of my mind, too. When in the course of events my mother became old and bed-ridden I went to considerable expense to have her transferred to a comfortable home up in London, so that I could visit her regularly. After that, somehow, the letters to Karen became fewer and fewer, until they stopped altogether.

It was nearly ten years before I saw the Cove again. They had been ten highly successful years for me. I had worked my way through several high class agencies, picking the brains of some of the best men in the business, and two years ago I had joined in with a couple of other enterprising advertising executives to start an agency of our own. We had each managed to bring with us a number of valuable accounts, and since then we had expanded rapidly. I had a four figure income of respectable proportions, a luxurious office with fitted carpet, modern tubular desk and all the latest business equipment, a secretary of my own, a flat in Chelsea – and a fiancée called Brenda, who had been a copy-writer at one of the previous agencies and now worked for us, a girl as smooth and streamlined as one of our best advertisements, intelligent and attractive and a pleasure to be seen with. I was a lucky man, I knew, and my friends kept telling me, and it was a recognised thing that sooner or later we would be married. In the meantime we led a very social life among sophisticated and successful business people like ourselves, a round of luncheons and cocktail parties, theatres and dinners and chic restaurants.

It was a sudden, almost blind urge to escape from all this that brought me to the Cove again. The days were long and hot and London seemed all at once to be incredibly stuffy. I had a nostalgic vision of the Cove as I had once known it, seen from the top of the moors, the little grey cottages dropping steeply down to the restless sea – and I felt I wanted to go there.

Brenda wasn't very keen, really. She would have preferred the South of France, Nice or Menton, somewhere a little more sophisticated. But I suppose she sensed my inner determination for she gave in with good grace. When the train ran along the edge of Mount's Bay, with its vast glittering sheet of waters out of which rose the ghostly outline of St

Michael's Mount, she was even favourably impressed. All the same, knowing her tastes, I did not like to risk staying at the tiny pub above the Cove, and instead booked rooms at the largest and most metropolitan-style hotel in Penzance.

It was a couple of days before finally I managed to get Brenda to the Cove. First she had insisted on doing the more obvious sight-seeing trips, to St Ives and Mousehole and Lamorna, and Land's End itself. Unfortunately the visit to Land's End had been ruined by one of those thick Cornish mists and altogether Brenda was already a little disappointed with the holiday. In Juan-les-Pins, she pointed out, we could have been lying in the sun all day long.

The sun wasn't exactly glaring down when we came into the Cove, but at least there was no mist. It was what might be called a medium sort of day, the sky a blend of grey clouds and streaky blue – an effect that became fascinating if you studied it closely. In this kind of light, too, the Cove acquired a strange glow of its own that rather suited the quiet granite background.

I tried to explain this to Brenda, but she was not impressed. I suppose she had already made up her mind that this holiday was not for her, and I could not really blame her. I had probably talked at length about my old days at the Cove, and this had not helped. At any rate before we had done more than take a look at the harbour she announced she was tired and wanted to go back to the hotel. This seemed to me unreasonable and I said so, and the ensuing acrimonious discussion was the nearest two level-headed sophisticated people like us would ever get to a row. We settled it in the most sensible way by Brenda getting on the returning bus, while I promised to come along on the next bus in a couple of hours' time.

When Brenda had gone I immediately felt guilty about my lack of consideration. After all why should I expect her to be interested in the Cove, or my sentimental whims? The things I admired about Brenda, I recognised, had nothing to do with this sort of world, yet they were valid and important things. And yet ...

And yet, I knew there must be some purpose to my coming

back after all this time. Looking back I could see that for a long time now, many months, a year perhaps, I had been feeling increasingly restless and dissatisfied about something or other – about the pace of life, about the superficial way time was filled, about where everything was leading – maybe most of all about myself. Somehow nothing seemed to be worth caring about any more, I felt a deep sense of frustration.

Now that I had come back to this faraway place of my childhood, of my formative years, this feeling suddenly seemed to gather all around me. I remembered, vividly, those other years, and all that other restlessness that had conspired to carry me away to London. But I did not feel happy at the memory, I just felt confused.

Somehow I could not bring myself to call on the people who might have remembered me. Instead I took the cobbled path that climbed steeply out of the Cove to the granite cliff-top where so often I used to play as a child. There I walked out to the point and lay face downwards looking down on what had once been my whole world. At least the afternoon sunshine had broken through, lighting up all the secretive corners and bringing a hint of new life. I looked down upon the tiny harbour and the bobbing boats and the sandy beach, and all at once I was overcome by a kind of pain that seemed to rise up and permeate the whole of me, my body, my mind and my spirit.

Just at that moment someone stirred on the beach below, a woman who had been sitting with two children. The children, a boy and a girl, quickly moved, too, and began playing a game of romping around with their mother, racing here and there, whirling round and round. I could hear their thin, piping cries of excitement rising up on the afternoon air, and then even above them the voice of their mother: and all at once, so that my heart almost stopped still, I knew that it was Karen's voice. An older, rather more solid Karen, I fancied, but still, I could imagine from my perch a million miles away, the same bright-eyed, grave-faced Karen with whom I had once walked the cliff tops.

As I watched, Karen bent to collect her things, and then called the children and began walking slowly across the harbour beach towards the high wall that broke the incoming sea. As she did so I spied for the first time, as she must have done, the tall mast of one of the fishing boats returning from a trip. The boat was painted blue and black, with a great red sail that billowed in the wind as it rounded the outer point of the harbour, then glided gently to its moorings.

Almost before it happened I knew that the man whom Karen had married would be on that boat, and that as he climbed wearily up the iron ladder to the quayside Karen and his two children would be waiting there to welcome him back. And somehow I knew too, without ever quite being able to see, that as they turned and walked back arm in arm through the Cove there would be something about Karen, a kind of glow of happiness, so that anyone who saw her would feel like saying, as I had once said, 'Why, you look like summertime ... like summertime.'

I stayed a long time on the cliffs looking down at the Cove that afternoon, looking at the mirror of all that might have been, and all that I had really lost ... I knew that I would never see the Cove again, but that it was important I had come back just this once – perhaps to find something I had lost. If I had my life all over again I knew that I would never have left the Cove and Karen – never, never, oh never! But then, we do not have our lives over again.

I caught the bus back to Penzance, and the next morning I took Brenda back to London. She hadn't said much since the previous afternoon, but now as the train rattled steadily and inevitably over the points I watched her thoughtfully as she stared out of the window. She had a fine face, Brenda, an open and frank face, a face that had courage and honesty. Suddenly she must have felt my gaze upon her: she turned and looked across at me, and, a little uncertainly, we smiled at one another. With a sudden gesture I leaned forward and took her hand in mine.

'Brenda,' I said, speaking perhaps more earnestly and humbly than ever before in all my life. 'When we get back – let's get married soon, shall we?'

IX

Passenger to Penzance

When, after eluding the grasp of an irate ticket collector and sprinting at full speed down half the length of Plymouth station, I managed to bundle into the very last compartment of the afternoon London-Penzance express, my first inclination was to collapse into a comfortable corner seat and gulp back some of the precious wind I had lost.

It was only as the train gathered speed and was rattling through the suburbs that I looked up and saw there was another passenger in the compartment, occupying the far corner seat. Even then it needed a second startled half-incredulous look before I realised that the passenger, a stout middle-aged business man, was huddled in his corner in a most unnatural position – his clothes torn and dishevelled, his face a mass of bruises and cuts, a thin line of blood trickling out of the corner of his mouth.

I threw down my suitcase and leapt over to the man, feeling I must do something, I loosened his collar and gingerly propped his lolling head in a more comfortable position. With my handkerchief I dabbed at the trickle of blood.

'Thank you,' said the man, hissing the words rather than speaking them, his swollen lips hardly moving. 'It's good of you to want to help me. But I'm afraid it's really no use. Apart from the damage so apparent to you I should mention that I have several ribs broken, possibly a broken collarbone – and a slight matter of a knife wound in my back.'

Still more aghast, I put my arm under his shoulder and felt a rough hole in the cloth of his coat. It was wet and sticky; my fingers, when I looked at them, were stained with blood.

Seeing the blood oozing again out of the man's mouth I dabbed at it with my handkerchief.

'I am dying – not slowly, but quickly,' said the man, trying to get the words out as if in a race against menacing oblivion.

I put my hand on his head. I didn't know what else to do.

'So,' continued the man, between pauses for breath. 'So, the problem, the only thing remaining, is how to avoid implicating you in an affair which has really nothing to do with you. The journey to Penzance will not take long. The communication cord is cut. You have no way of getting out unless you open the door and jump out – and I wouldn't advise that. We will have to think fast. But first I had better explain how all this has come about.

'The fact is that I have been attacked – by an old enemy of mine. He appeared at the carriage door while the train was standing at Exeter, got in and attacked me – with the results you see. It was all over in a few minutes, with no one the wiser. I must have fainted, or became unconscious. During the remainder of the time I imagine he sat by the window and frowned away anybody else who looked like getting in the carriage. He himself must have jumped out just as the train moved. He could not have bargained on yourself making a last-minute dash and boarding the train when it was already moving. He probably reckoned that by the time my body was found on arrival at Penzance it would be as near as could be impossible for the police to trace who was responsible.'

There was another silence. When the man resumed talking it was with considerably more difficulty.

'Excuse my slowness,' he said. 'Dying is not a comfortable business – even in the best of circumstances, I imagine.'

'You are facing it very bravely, sir,' I said well-meaningly.

'Thanks ... Where are we now?'

We were slipping through quiet country, but on the horizon there were signs of rooftops.

'We must be approaching Liskeard,' I said. 'But we don't stop there.'

'Still, we have to hurry. Listen to me carefully ... For you to be found here on arrival at Penzance, would be both dangerous and futile.'

I motioned weakly with my hands. 'But – perhaps – a doctor – I could have you rushed to hospital – '

'Please – you're wasting time. This train doesn't stop before we reach Penzance, which means there is absolutely no way out for you. You can't get out of the carriage. The only alternative, then, is for *me* to get out.'

I stared. 'But how ...?'

The voice trembled.

'In a few moments, a very few moments, I shall be dead. It's no use wasting words about it ... This is what I want you to do. Wait till we have passed through Liskeard and are out into open country again. When you are quite sure the train is passing through a fairly isolated part – push me out through the door.'

'Oh!' I ejaculated, in instinctive horror.

The eye-lids flickered with irritation at my squeamishness. A speck of blood fell on the man's crumpled shirt front.

'Don't-be-a-fool! It's the only way.' He took a sudden heavy breath. 'It – frees you from all implication. By the time my body is discovered, and its connection with this train traced, you will have vanished. It will be too late for the police to do anything.'

'But – ' I wanted to say something to protest if only to satisfy my conscience. But there seemed to be nothing I could say.

'No buts ...' The voice suddenly weakened, tailed away. 'No buts. Do-as-I-say.'

I bent down. 'But – have you no messages? Don't you want me to tell anyone? What about your relatives? – Are you married?'

My urgent questions went unanswered, the words echoing hollowly in a sudden loneliness that filled the carriage. I looked closer at the blood-speckled face. It seemed suddenly still. The eyes were closed with a suggestion of finality. I felt for the man's pulse, pressing my fingers deep into the flesh of his wrist. There was no movement.

The buildings of Liskeard loomed on each side of the speeding train like menacing shadows. Startled out of my shock by this new danger, I quickly sat down beside the dead man, leaning forward slightly so that if anyone should chance to look into the carriage as we went through the station they would see only myself. In this manner we ran safely on towards open country again: past Lostwithiel, Par and St Austell.

The precious minutes were slipping by. I looked out at the grey houses of passing villages, and wished that I could change places with any of the occupants. I looked up at the torn communication cord. What the man had said was frighteningly correct. To attract attention would be the worst possible thing. I looked at the man again; neat, well-dressed, surrounded by an air of prosperity; now sprawling incongruously in his corner seat: suddenly such a vital part of my life, yet such a stranger, such a mystery. On an impulse, I began to search his pockets. They were empty of any clue to his identity. His luggage, if he had any was gone.

It was hopeless, fantastic, inexplainable ... I looked out of the window, seeing peaceful country landscapes again, we were somewhere just beyond Truro, but I knew that before long – and then the ultimate panic swept over me, the panic of self-preservation that makes ordinary people murder, thieve and tell lies, and perform acts that would normally be beyond them.

With a swift movement I bent down and got my shoulder into the pit of the dead man's stomach. Grunting at the effort, I slowly raised him out of the seat. Moving one foot at a time in order to keep balance with the swaying of the train, I tottered to the compartment door. With a jerk of my knee I lifted the handle and the door swung open, caught by the rushing wind. For a moment I stood poised, watching the gold and green colours swirling by. Then, awkwardly, I tumbled the body out through the opening. I watched it fall into thick grass and roll down the slope.

It seemed ages before the train edged in under the great dusty dome of Penzance station, yet I did nothing but sit, tense with horror. As I rose to my feet my eyes were drawn again to the spot where the man had been sitting. On the floor there was a small dark pool! the blood was still dripping in slow drops from the edge of the cushioned seat. I looked from the floor to the cushion. As if mesmerised, I looked down at myself. There was blood on my coat, on my shoes, on my trousers. My clothes were disarranged from the effort of throwing the man out of the train. They held an obvious connection with the general dishevelment of the carriage, the many evidences that a struggle had taken place.

Before the train had come to a stop I opened the door and jumped out, ignoring the remonstrance of a porter. I wanted only to get out and away into the safe anonymity of the local streets. Discarding any pretence at normality I hurried to the barrier, thrust my ticket at the collector and half-ran out of the station. As I went I fancied I saw a porter opening the door of my carriage. It could be as quick as that, I thought in alarm.

I didn't bother about my business in Penzance that afternoon. For a time I walked about the streets, wondering whether there was any way in which I could inform the police that a man had been murdered. But I realised more forcibly than ever how impossible that had become. Next I went into a public wash-place and scrubbed my hands. As I was putting on my coat again I saw the attendant eyeing it queerly, his eyes dropping to the blood-stains on my trousers.

That settled it. I caught the next bus over to Hayle. There I wandered through the side streets until I found a second-hand clothes shop. I managed to purchase an old suit and an older raincoat, and with these tucked under my arm I set off along the sands. When I had gone far enough to be out of sight of stray walkers I went behind a sand-dune, took off my own suit and put on the second-hand clothes. My own clothes I buried in the sand, pushing them deep down. Then, though feeling in no way more secure for all my efforts, I walked back into Hayle and caught a bus again to Penzance.

When I arrived at Penzance it was getting late. I went to an hotel and booked in, taking care – with the seemingly automatic ingenuity that is given to the newest criminal – to make it well-known that I had just arrived in the town. I ordered a meal and a stiff whisky to be sent up to my room. While waiting I went for a stroll around the hotel block. On the way, prompted by some twinge of curiosity, I bought an evening newspaper. But when I got up to my room I was by this time aching with hunger. Only when I was reasonably satisfied by the meal and the drink did I sink back into an armchair and open out the paper.

I hardly expected to see anything so soon about the afternoon's occurrence, but my eyes were at once caught by the heading of one of the front-page stories. WELL-KNOWN PENZANCE BUSINESS MAN THROWN FROM TRAIN. I read on, uneasily. The opening paragraph was more than enough. It said:

> A well-known Penzance estate agent, Mr Alexander Smith, was today thrown out of his compartment on a London-Penzance express train, just before the train reached the outskirts of Penzance. Although the train was travelling at about 50 miles per hour, Mr Smith was uninjured save for minor cuts and abrasions. His fall was seen by men working in nearby fields and he was quickly rushed to the local hospital where he was stated this evening to be progressing very well. In an interview with the police, Mr Smith stated that he was suddenly attacked by a young man who was the only other occupant of his carriage. Before he could make any effective resistance he had been lifted up and thrown out of the carriage. Mr Smith is convinced that he would recognise his assailant again. Meanwhile the police are making wide inquiries, and are particularly anxious to trace a young man who was seen to jump from the train when it reached Penzance, and make a hurried exit from the station. It is believed he may have some knowledge of the crime.

The same night, half an hour later, I checked hurriedly out of the hotel. I could feel looming around me a huge circle of burly painstaking policemen, each one methodically following up his little task of investigation, each one carefully building the unshakable foundations of a fantastic mountain of accusation – each one ferreting out his proud discovery, the lavatory attendant who remembered attending a certain young man, the bus conductress who remembered selling a ticket to Hayle to a certain young man, the second-hand clothes dealer who remembered disposing of an old suit and a raincoat to a certain young man, the hotel clerk who remembered booking a room to a certain young man ...

I caught a bus to Truro slept the night there, got up early and caught a train back to my home in London. My father and mother were surprised to see me: I hadn't been due back for some days. I told them I was off on another job, a long job, and didn't know when I would be back. I changed my clothes again, packed a suitcase, gave the old clothes to my mother and told her to be sure to burn them. I said they weren't to tell my sister or anyone else that I'd been back. If any strange men called they were to say I'd been away for weeks and they didn't know where I was. If anyone asked if I'd been in Penzance on such and such a date the answer was NO. My mother and father looked at me queerly, their eyes reflecting the struggle between anxiety and suspicion. Soon, I reflected, the snowball would catch them up, take them bounding along with it, poisoning their minds with an endless stream of unanswerable questions.

I said goodbye and walked out of the house and down the road. On the corner I bought a newspaper. The Stop Press carried a paragraph headed 'Penzance Train Attack'. It said that the police had received important information from a local bus conductress who remembered ... I hailed a taxi and disappeared into the maze of London. I had begun moving on.

I have been moving on ever since. For over a week I wandered about London, trying to lose myself; but always, wherever I went, I felt uneasy, haunted by the sight of policemen. They stood on corners, or hidden in shop entrances, or simply moved ponderously along their beat.

Next I went to Wales. Then through the Midlands.

Wherever I went I kept myself buried in anonymity, eating in cheap cafes, sleeping in lodging-houses, in air-raid shelters, sometimes in fields. Once or twice, while I still had a fair amount of money left, I tried staying at hotels, but each time something in the way the clerk looked at me made me clear out. I became more and more sensitive to the way people looked at me, no matter how innocently. I came to feel nervous immediately when someone looked in my direction. Then, my only thought would be flight, swift effacement of my self without waiting for any questions, without making any challenge.

I am never able to stay more than a few days in one place. I can never forget the growing snowball of suspicion and incrimination which is bearing down on me. There is no need for me to find out whether the search is still on. I know, implicitly, that it is. Each time I move on I take the most detailed precautions to obliterate my traces. But each time, unwittingly, I leave another clue. Looking back I imagine, so vividly, the questing finger coming out of the darkness, pouncing on the clue, storing it away – the scrap of paper with my name on it, the specimen of hand-writing, the unguarded remark to a waiter. And always, at the back of it all, I sense the ultimate, the frightening climax.

'Mr Smith is convinced he would recognise his assailant again.' Could he? Would he?

It should be so simple, so easy to prove or disprove. I have only to go to Penzance, to make straight for a certain estate agent's office. I have only to walk through a common-place frosted glass door, bearing the name Mr Alexander Smith. I tell myself I *will* go – now, today, this morning, this afternoon. I force myself to prepare for the journey: I set out for a station, or to get a bus. But always my footsteps falter, hesitate, turn back. I am stopped always by one thing, an idea looming in front of me like a towering and by now insurmountable wall.

With each passing day I find it increasingly difficult to decide which story is the true one – mine, or Alexander Smith's.

X

The Last Day

A speck on the bright glassiness of an ocean, the man sprawled awkwardly across the narrow confinements of his raft. He was half-propping himself up on one elbow, and the bottom of it pressed firmly on a sheet of notepaper, stained yellow from contact with water and sun. In his other hand the man held a small blue pencil stump, tapping one end in a steady rhythm against the hard wood surface of the raft. The continuous tapping had bored a tiny groove into the wood and every now and then this caught the sunlight and winked up, unexpectedly, like a black, beady eye. The occasional reflection, seeming almost to be a spark of life, had begun to fascinate the man. At first he had tapped idly, as a background to the thoughts occupying his attention. Now his thoughts were more elusive and he found himself concentrating on the task of tapping the pencil point precisely over the same spot, so that the eye grew large and round, the wink brighter and more lifelike. By this process he was systematically blunting the pencil point, and there would be no means of sharpening it again. Perhaps this warning thought, pricking at some faraway corner of his mind, accounted for a vague frown that brooded across the man's thin, hair-stubbled face. The more he tapped, the more pronounced became the annoyed creases between his eyes, the slight irritable droop of the mouth; yet some childish obstinacy made him continue. It was as if he wished to experience both the torture and the sensual ecstasy of pursuing a wasteful, even harmful activity, while conscious of its dangers.

He had had the pencil and notepaper from the time of the shipwreck, but this was the first occasion he had become aware that they might serve some useful purpose. Hitherto, they had remained stuffed away in the pocket of his windswept, sea-drenched trousers, along with a ring, a loose button and an old postage stamp, all of which had seemed equally useless. He had been far more interested in his other possessions: some dry ship biscuits, a small tin of corned beef, a bar of chocolate, a cylinder of fresh water – and a waterproof matchbox, containing half a dozen matches. He did not quite know why he attached such importance to the matchbox, but he felt a blind faith in its potential power of achievement. He kept the box wedged solidly between two of the raft logs, regarding it worshippingly as a sort of ultimate miracle worker.

Beside the matchbox, the pencil and the crumpled sheet of paper seemed particularly important. So, too, did the other fragments, including the tattered half-remains of a shirt and trousers that clung to his bony body. The most real and important things had been the food and drink. He had divided them and juggled with them, but with each long burning day they had dwindled. Now they were no longer real in fact, though ever present and extremely vivid in his imagination. He had sucked down the last crumb of biscuit about three days previously, and the same afternoon he had let the last drop of water dribble slowly along his thickened lips, into the dry hollow of his mouth.

Since then he had lain helplessly on the raft, listening to the endless toneless murmur of the waves against the sides, feeling the sharp warmth of the sun burning a thousand pinpricks into his chest. Sometimes, laboriously, he had wriggled over on to his face, letting the burning parts of his body sink gratefully against the cool sea-washed limbs of the raft. But then, after a while, the heat on his back had become equally intolerable, sending strange pains shooting through his body, down to the very nerve centres. It would have been possible to alleviate the torture by adopting different positions, but he knew, without the attempt, that the pinpoint of energy remaining within him would expire before more than a handful of those positions had been attained. Even night brought little relief, for then there was a sudden damp, uncomfortable coolness, against which his flimsy clothes offered no protection... the contrasting temperatures left him shivering, hot flushes burning in his cheeks, across his forehead. Yet to move was agony. So he lay spreadeagled, relaxing himself completely, letting the pains and the flames do what they willed, but maintaining, somehow — through the hot mists that obscured his eyes — a half-contact with life, with the vast horizon of sea and sun and sky and nothingness.

But today — early, while the sun's warmth was still friendly — the man on the raft was fighting stubbornly to retain consciousness. His mind, wandering in a nether-world for three days, had captured, out of the blankness, an idea. Now, alone, drained of the most elemental cravings, the man became aware of a tremendous urge, almost a spiritual urge; an urge to communicate, to express something that was within him. It was something that had been growing up inside, with each long hour of his suffering, and which he now desired, with an excruciating wistfulness, to create into something tangible, something visible. In his mind the words floated about vaguely, beyond his control, every now and then threatening to vanish into a terrifying void. He had tried to give them voice, to give them the meaning of sound... but when he moved his sore swollen lips there was no sound, only the whistle of air in his throat. Then he remembered the forlorn piece of paper and the pencil stump.

It required a considerable effort to get them out of his pocket and to find a position suitable for writing (the shirt turned up over the back of his neck and head to give temporary relief from the sun). He lay diagonally across the raft in order to balance it against any possible rocking by the waves — though today, as nearly every day, the sea was as smooth as a mirror. Fitting the paper over a smooth part of the wood, he lifted his elbow over it and twisted his body into the least unbearable position. It all took time. And then, at last, when he was ready, the little pencil fixed tightly between his fingers, he found himself suddenly struck with panic at the sight of the vast blank sheet of paper. He could not think what to do with the pencil point when it reached the beginning of that huge plain of emptiness. At last, tired of poising the pencil in mid-air, he let it dive down, disconsolately, into the woodwork. And, jabbing away, he created the black beady eye – only for it to grow into compelling reality, becoming an accuser, mocking his inaction.

The man wanted to write. Part of him, remembering faraway disciplines and codes, struggled with a jumble of facts and figures: the date and cause of the shipwreck, the approximate longitude and latitude, a day-by-day log of the period afloat, a list of 'equipment' on the raft. He realised that these were things a dutiful sailor would have noted down on the first day. But the first day, and the second day and the day after that and the day after that and the day after that, his mind had been occupied completely with certain vital, immediate things. Food and water, the mood of the sea, the inhuman heat of the sun, the problem of himself – the dull ache in his groin, the occasional heaving of his chest, the thickening veins standing out grotesquely. Now even these things were ceasing to have any clarity in his life. They, like the odd, catalogued facts – biscuits, water, a box of matches – were only so many meaningless puppets, dancing endless jigs in the back of his mind.

He remembered the simple trivial things one wrote about on the ordinary, routine sea trip. The weather, the people on board, the book one had been reading, the game of cards, the prospects for leave. Then the comfortable routine of life was taken for granted, now it had become unreal. Only this was real. Yet he felt no desire, indeed an incapacity, to write about this – the raft eight feet by twelve, the hot days and the cold nights, the queer itinerary of possessions (the biscuit he had broken into four pieces, and then into eight, making each piece a meal). How could he write about – what would be the meaning of? – the other survivor, the woman with the slit-open head, dying in the night, her body crumpled up in a queer attitude of prayer, becoming something ethereal, so that he did not dare to touch her? (In the end, furtively, the next night, he pushed his weight up and down against one side of the raft. He heard a faint slither but no splash, as if the sea had opened out its arms to take in its child. In the morning there were only the bare, uncommunicative logs of the raft.) It would have been possible to write about water, about how one held the water flask at an acutely judged angle, so that the water came out in single round drops, each drop splashing first on to the dry lips, then oozing into the mouth, spreading out in a cool, wondrous caress. How, though it was three days and nights since the last drop disappeared, he could still hold the flask up and see, as if it was real, a great blob of water dangling, hesitating, trembling. How he found himself with crackled lips involuntarily parted, tongue tip pointing out, waiting, waiting, waiting ... (and all around him the cool forbidden pool). No, he could no more write about these things than about unreal facts and figures. Not now, with the empty flask beside him, the smell of vanished biscuits lingering.

It came upon the man gradually, what he wanted to write, like a small misty vision. It came upon him along with the hot dry feverishness, the pain beyond pain, the sense of beginning to float out of himself and into space. More than ever before in his life he felt the urgency to get this one thing out of him, to compress his whole being and expression into some final, illuminating truth, a meaning for his life.

For a long long time the man lay still, thinking, his eyes half-closed. Then, gradually, the frown slackened its grip on his face, the crinkles between his eyes straightened. He opened his eyes, and they were round and gleaming. He began writing.

There was nothing easy or flowing about his writing. The words floated about in his mind like fish in the sea, each one representing a considerable effort of capture. Even when he was sure of a word he had tremendous difficulty in committing it to the paper. As he wrote each word he kept repeating it to himself over and over again, as if it was a magic thing. It took him half an hour to complete the first two lines.

Exhausted, the man turned on his side. Above him the sun swam high in the sky like a strange flaming balloon. It was an uncomfortable heat now; at the feel of it his limbs gave tiny quivers, as if struck with ague. He could feel the heat eating into him, burrowing through the raw exterior of his flesh into the very heart of him. Sometimes it seemed to him that the entire energies of the sun were concentrated on blistering him out of existence. He had long ago accepted the inevitability of it all. He felt, instinctively, that he had already left the world beyond the horizon of the bare shimmering sea. He could no longer believe in the existence of clouds, of rain, of dull skies ... only the sun, hating him.

Turning over on his face again, he resumed his laboured writing. He worked at an even slower rate, partly because what he wished to say involved a greater difficulty in expression, partly because he was forced to pause at increasingly frequent intervals, in order to force his mind and his drowsing limbs back from an enticing oblivion. But he kept on, his being held together by the compulsion of this single task which could not be left uncompleted. He wrote with the pencil stump at an angle, the only way in which he could get any marking out of the blunted point. He held the pencil between the tip of his first finger and the tip of his thumb, held it unnaturally and precariously. The pencil rolled about drunkenly as he pushed it laboriously up and down, or traced it round in a wobbling curve. It began to seem to him that the letters and words were no longer static, but had started moving about like vague shadows, even as he wrote. Once he had the extraordinary feeling that the paper had merged into the wood of the raft, and only reassured himself by tracing with the tip of his finger the rough, crinkling surface.

Nearing the end of the page he felt the strength suddenly flowing away from him, and he tried desperately to push the swaying pencil faster and faster to the end of its journey. He jabbed down the last words in erratic straggling lines, wavering along the very bottom edge of the paper. He was still staring at them wonderingly when he had the surprising sensation that the sea was rising up in a gigantic spray. It began rolling over him in long soothing movements, and he felt himself bobbing about like a cork. His face fell forward on to the notepaper, dry lips pressing into the coarse surface. His eyes were closed. Slowly his hand slipped over the side of the raft and dangled half in the sea; but by some miracle the pencil remained gripped tight between his fingers.

When the man on the raft regained consciousness the sea was as before, quiet, shimmering and sleeping. But the sun had sailed far across the sky and dropped low into its western corner. The red sinking rays were vanishing behind the heavy shadows of dusk.

At first he remained in a half-daze, remembering nothing, conscious only of an unbelievable pain that seemed to be devouring the whole of his body, leaping out like a flame to every limb. The pain even curled over his eyelids, weighing them down, so that it needed an intense physical effort to force them open. It was when he had done so, when he found himself looking out into the brown shapelessness of dusk, that the tiny arrow of remembrance pierced into his consciousness, as vivid and startling as the first ache of pain. At the same time he felt an odd sense of alarm, or urgency. He groped about with his fingers. Yes, the paper was still there, harsh and crinkly against his cheek. And then, realising with cold clarity why he was alarmed, he raised his head and looked down. The piece of paper swam before him like a white ghost, merging into the blanket of dusk. He could not read a word of what he had written.

For some time the man stared at the paper. It became for him a thing alone, complete, devouring his whole attention. Confronted by its unexpected secretiveness he felt incapable of any action other than glaring down at it through the grey swirling shadows. His eyes strained to pierce the cloak of dullness until they twitched and blinked with hot pain. In his desperate attempts to see he bent his face down over the paper so that its surface brushed against his eyelashes – that failing, he raised his head and held the paper up against the sky, hoping that a dying ray of sun might light up the words. But the sun sank into its sleep with the same pitiless disdain as in daytime.

The man began crying, slow wondering tears that trickled saltily across his cheeks. In vain he tried to remember the words he had created. Set down on to the paper they seemed to have escaped from him forever. Yet they were his, of him, were his creation; in them was bound up his achievement, his fulfilment. He groaned and pressed his aching forehead deep into the raft logs until the cold wetness threatened to hurtle him into oblivion again. Rolling his head from side to side he began twisting one hand, in a gesture of intolerable anguish, across the surface of the raft. And as he did so his fingers, clawing out in a last convulsion of frustration, touched the small sharp corners of the waterproof matchbox, tucked between two logs.

For several moments the man fingered the box, fingers slowly tracing out the meaning of their discovery. Then, as understanding flooded up his arm and into his mind, his fingers closed possessively, triumphantly, around the matchbox. He pulled it from its hiding place and brought it close under his bent face. With one fumbling trembling finger he began poking out the inner compartment.

He took out a match, holding it gently, almost lovingly. Once he had dreamed of lighting a match in answer to some miraculous faraway rescuing signal. Now he knew that it had been reserved for a greater, more supreme purpose. Cupping the box in his other hand, he struck the match hard against the side. There was a familiar tearing sound, a minute spark, but no flame. Gathering all his strength he struck again. Abruptly, the red, mauve-tinged flame shot out of nothingness. It flickered uncertainly for a moment then, sheltered deep in the man's hand, settled into a warm, friendly glow. By it he saw, suddenly alive and revealed, the crumpled paper.

The man gave a tiny sigh and bent forward, his lips curling back to spell out each silent but potent word. The paper trembled before him, but with a tremendous concentration he focused it squarely into the light of the match. His eyes recognised the familiar background of faded stains, the long watery creases. Then, in a rising, possessive ecstasy he began reading, mumbling words to himself as a halting but joyous prayer, mumbling, mumbling, mumbling.

Later the last match flickered out and in the embracing darkness the man sank forward until his face pressed sadly against the hard, dark wood of the raft. Later a sea wave caught up the man's limp hand and swung it to one side so that it lay awash with the green water, each wave licking greedily at the tiny scrap of paper that was still clutched tight between clenched fingers. Later, the sheet of paper became a nonsensical pattern of black lines that climbed up into mountains and plunged down into caverns, that sprawled into ungainly shapes and cramped into furtive corners — lines that had no beginning and no ending on that sheet of paper, so that no one else could know whether they ever existed or had meaning.

But the man knew, at the end of his day, and so it ever is, and all that matters.

XI

The Woman on the Couch

The woman as Edwards first saw her, as he was always to see her, lay on a couch by the front sitting room window, her head propped up by a mountain of green and gold cushions so that she could look out through discreet lace curtains upon the dahlias and the rhododendrons, the carefully trimmed laurel bushes, beyond them the unchanging pattern of Llanglos Street and its neat red brick villas. Tucked discreetly above the couch was the steel post and the elongated arm fitted with the rope pulley. When there was a visitor or a meal or some outside event worth closer attention, or simply when to lie flat on the back became quite unbearable, the pulley enabled the cripple to pull herself up to a sitting position. Then she would seem to become (but not quite) part of the normal architecture of a sitting room: couches, armchairs, an ornamental mirror, flowers on the table – one or two human beings, bodies arched in the everyday activities of talking or perhaps eating.

For those familiar with the scene there might sometimes even be the illusion of normality. But for strangers, for Edwards at first, there could not be that illusion. His eyes could not escape the fascination of the trailing pulley, the stark but expressive steel post, the whole dishevelled geography of the couch; above all the disturbing personality of the woman with the paralysed legs, alive only from the waist upwards.

When he first came to the house he remained for some time unaware of this strange reclusive occupant. He wanted a bed sitting room and someone at the newspaper office gave him the address. When he knocked the door was opened by Mrs Simmons, stout and bustling, white hair loose and untidy, still in curlers. He assumed her to be the proprietress. She showed him to the only available room, on the top floor with a view out over roof tops to the distant sea. It was a small room, but neat and tidy; there was a gas fire and a table and armchair, a comfortable old-fashioned feather bed; it would suit his purposes admirably. When he told Mrs Simmons that he had come to work as a reporter on the *Evening Telegraph* she was impressed and seemed pleased that he decided to take the room. She showed him the bathroom and the dining-room where meals were served, gave him a glimpse into the kitchen and took him round the back of the house to introduce him to her husband, a wiry foxy-faced old man who seemed entirely absorbed in his gardening. But she made no reference to her daughter and she did not draw his attention to the front sitting-room. It was actually several days before, passing the door on his way home after work, he became aware of the presence within the room of a human being. He stood listening and caught the sound of gentle breathing, but some instinct made him hesitate from probing further, and he went on upstairs.

Then, coming out of the dining-room one evening, he noticed a light showing in the mysterious room, and the door ajar. At that moment, so naturally that he was hardly surprised a voice called out: 'Come in, Mr Edwards.'

When he went in he found most of the room in the shadow but the area around the couch was illuminated by the light of four tall red candles. In this flickering glow the couch became a soft landscape of colours and braided patterns against which was posed, as if for a portrait, the reclining figure of the crippled woman. At first he hardly noticed the figure, most of it buried into a heap of rugs, for his eyes were compelled towards the long white face, half shrouded by a glorious mass of reddy-gold hair. The deep red of the hair, the accentuated pallor of the skin, gave the face a suggestion of supernatural beauty; the hollows of the cheekbones and the strained lines under the eyes, the narrow, embittered twist of the lips, were not noticed. When Edwards, normally an acute observer, began to notice he also saw the pulley and the blankets, and comprehension brought upon him the inevitable flood of conventional pity.

'How do you do, Mr Edwards. My name is Miriam Simmons. I don't suppose my mother has seen occasion to mention me. She likes to pretend as far as possible that I am neatly tucked away, the minimum fuss and bother.'

'How do you do,' he said awkwardly.

'My mother tells me you've taken the top room. I hope you find it comfortable?'

'Yes, quite comfortable.'

'And everything else to your satisfaction?'

'Thank you, yes.'

He found himself inclining to turn his gaze away. Ashamed, he forced his eyes to meet the other's. Her eyes, he noticed, were very large and slightly protruding, seeming to swell with a power and energy denied to the body.

'The top room has the best view. I hope you find it a good atmosphere for writing?'

Edwards raised his eyebrows.

'How did you – ?'

The woman on the couch made a languid gesture, a faint gleam of amusement flickering across her eyes.

'You told my mother that you were working for the *Telegraph*. She reports impressive piles of typing paper on your desk. And the faint drumming of your typewriter floats down here every now and then – it's rather a pleasant sound.' She chuckled drily. 'I am by nature a most inquisitive person. Circumstances, which as you see combine to immobilise me, only intensify the ardour of my curiosity. Other people's lives, everything about them – it's all fuel for the insatiable fire. So it's natural enough that I should gobble up every little piece of news about life, glamorous life, within this particular cog in the chain of cogs they call Llanglos Street.'

Her voice as she spoke seemed to develop a hard, almost metallic edge. What might have been meant as bantering became harsh and bitter. Edwards winced. Seeing this, she curled her lip sardonically.

'Perhaps you take an optimistic view of life, Mr Edwards? You can hardly blame me for being inclined in the opposite way.'

Edwards shrugged.

'That seems a pity. I should have thought – '

The head stirred, petulantly.

'Please don't moralise. Rather satisfy my curiosity. You are the first person to live here for years who seems to possess some intelligence and' – momentarily her eyes flickered uneasily at feeling their consideration of him – 'attractiveness. Come, tell me something about yourself, your writing. Don't you get rather bored with reporting council meetings and church bazaars?'

For the first time Edwards smiled.

'Naturally. But it happens to be my bread and butter. I have – other writing. Stories. Every journalist is this split person, one half of him writing his journalese, the other half secretly trying to use words as they should be used, creatively, excitingly.'

'Good, Mr Edwards, very good. Tell me some more.'

He found it easy, the first time, to talk. He talked for about an hour, and while he did so it seemed to him that there was a new flush of colour to her cheeks. All at once he felt himself quite tired, realised that he had almost exhausted himself, and his voice was hoarse.

'I must stop, I shall tire you,' he said hastily.

A frown flickered across the white forehead. She spoke almost irritably.

'No. Go on. Tell me more.'

But he felt drained of his energy, his vitality.

'No. I – must go.' He rose decisively. 'Perhaps another time – if it won't bore you.'

The woman looked up at him. For a moment he stared into her eyes seeing them growing larger and larger, like two round swimming planets, whirling in some strange universe. He had a strange sensation that they were pulling at him, that they were even trying to compel him to stay. It required a considerable effort of his will to break the gaze, to mumble some pleasantry and back out of the room.

After that Edwards became uncomfortably conscious of the sitting-room and its occupant. At first he was tempted to speak about Miriam to her mother, to the other boarders, to find out things about her life, what had happened to her, what she was before. But when he remembered the feeling of her eyes upon him, penetrating into the guards of his privacy, he grew frightened and wanted only to forget the whole affair. In this state of unease he found himself inclined, on coming down the stairs for a meal, to run across the hallway towards the safety of the breakfast-room, averting his eyes from the half-open door on his left. When he arrived home in the evenings he endeavoured to insert the key in the door with the minimum of noise, turning the handle in cautious silence and padding quickly and softly up to his room. There, looking out of his window and over to the far crooked line of the waves, or trying to lose himself in some intangible fragmentation of a story, he found a corner of his mind always remembering, uneasily, the little room downstairs. He tried to remind himself that this was a perfectly ordinary, suburban house, imbued with a perfectly ordinary suburban atmosphere and procedure. But he knew already that for him there was some tiny dark twist which, by its presence, had altered the whole shape and nature of the house, of his life.

Oh it was ridiculous, he told himself, allowing his mind to be dominated by this thought. Or rather, it was unworthy, unfair to Miriam, this giving way to a – a sense of distaste (as he assumed it to be). When he felt his sense of shame at its strongest he frowned and forced himself to go downstairs to tap on the door of the sitting-room.

She always received him nonchalantly, without surprise, almost as if she knew he would come. If it was evening she lay back against the rainbow contours of the couch; if it was daytime she moved nearer to the window, staring out dreamily upon the unchanging scene. One day turning into the garden, he felt her eyes upon him. He looked up and smiled rather nervously, having the sensation that as soon as he entered the square outline of her vision he became appropriated by her eyes, possessed by them. Once inside the door he ran up the stairs two at a time.

Their talking was spasmodic, unpredictable. Always he intended to ask her questions, to know about her, and always, it seemed, it was he who laid bare his life and all its intimacies. She seemed able, despite his strongest resolutions, to draw things out of him, and each time that he yielded he was aware of a greater sense of inferiority.

When he had been sitting with her and went away he noticed a curious exhilaration, a new nervous energy, and often, then, he would sit down at his table and write for two or three hours, far into the night. But after those few hours the strength left him, and seemed only renewable by visiting her again.

'It's strange, you seem quite an inspiration to my writing,' he said grudgingly, a little afraid even of the admission.

'Read me one of your stories,' she said quickly.

'Oh ... some other time. It would probably bore you.'

'You know it wouldn't. You're the first writer, I imagine, who ever refused an audience. And I don't suppose you really mean to.'

He laughed.

'You're right.'

He went upstairs, fetched his latest manuscript, came and sat down again on the chair facing the couch. She had thrown her hair back so that it hung over the back of the couch in cascading streams of red. Quite unconsciously he found his gaze shaping out the soft lines of her body under its camouflage of dressing-gown, of huddled rugs. He frowned. It was fantastic: a living beauty of half of a woman, a dead darkness for the rest of her. Without the one how could the other really exist? He repeated the thought to himself. He filled his mind with a great pity for this body doomed to lie there, for this body was was really dead. And then, as he glanced again, furtively, at the richness of the hair, the pallid beauty of the face, the gentle swell of the breasts – the pity faded drowned by a nervous excitement – for how could they not be alive? Could it be that in some strange way all the physical beauty that had been crushed in one part of this vision had merely been changed and focused in the other, unhurt part? He shook his head, irritably, as if to shake away such eerie thoughts, and began reading in a low voice.

It was quite a short story, about a man whose lover was drowned but came back to haunt him in dreams, and how eventually they found each other again by the man following her into the depths of the same cool lake. It was neither a bad nor a conspicuously successful story, yet as he read it in Miriam's presence it seemed to gain an entirely new quality, almost an added vibration. It was, he knew, something of his listener that was forcibly being added to the story, giving it a strength that he could not have given it. At the comprehension he felt weak and afraid.

When he had finished there was a silence. He heard her fumbling for a cigarette, shook his head as she motioned one towards him. She lit hers and blew a circle of smoke into the air. He watched it encircling his head.

'That's very good,' she said. 'That's far too good for a journalist.'

Now he did feel able to look, and saw her eyes quite soft and tender and knew, almost in a boyish way, that she had extracted more from the story than what was written. He felt as if she knew a great deal of his personality that she had not known before.

'My husband used to write,' she said, out of the silence.

He was startled.

'Husband?'

She smiled, a flicker of mockery crossing her face.

'Oh yes, I had a husband ... once. He was killed.'

'Oh I'm – I'm terribly sorry.'

'When this happened.' Her head nodded to the hidden, unreal part of her.

'I see.'

He ran his tongue round his mouth. He did not quite know what to say. But it was not from any conventional reticence. It was for quite a different reason. The reason was that after fighting against it for so long he now felt himself obsessed by a burning, unquenchable desire to know her, to enter her life.

'Was it – how – when did it happen?'

'Five years ago.' She spoke quite calmly, and all the time her eyes remained fixed on him, and he knew, without looking, that they were reassuring him. You shall know, they were saying. An immense relief flooded over him. He relaxed his body, his arms, his muscles, everything, including his mind, questioning nothing, giving himself up unreservedly to the acceptance of whatever she had to give him. He was untroubled by the slightest qualm or consideration about the breaking of his own defences, the unconscious offering of himself into her power.

'My husband was a Frenchman,' she went on. 'He spent a holiday here. That was how we met. We fell in love – at once.'

Somehow, as she spoke, he could imagine how they fell in love, how immediate and sweeping it had been. The husband remained a mystic, ghostly figure, a dark shadow. But he was profoundly aware of Miriam, he saw her walking beside the dark shadow, her arms brown and bare to the sun, her legs swaying backwards and forwards like any other lovely woman's legs, her body subtly vibrant with passion. There would have been no mildness, no half-heartedness about her falling in love, he thought, and shivered slightly.

'After we were married we went to live in France. Pierre had a good job – he worked for the Government, in the Department of Agriculture. Our home was in Paris, and we used to travel about the country by car, inspecting farms and research stations. Oh, the French country in spring – Brittany, Provence – it was wonderful. We used to have picnics, and bathe in the rivers. I was not a good swimmer, but Pierre soon taught me. He used to pull me in after him ...' Miriam smiled a slow, secret smile.

Now Edwards sunk his head and let his eyes fall upon the intricate pattern of the Turkish carpet, blue and red, gold Chinese dragon's teeth opened to grasp some unseen prey. His mouth had gone dry. He felt himself there, out in the sun-dried cornfields of France, beside her – aware of her warmth – desiring her youth, her ardent flesh – no, no, it was too much! He closed his lips together until they hurt from the pressure.

'And then one day, driving round a bend in a country lane we came upon a haycart drawn right across the road. We were travelling fast, much too fast. The car over-turned and burst into flames. Pierre – Pierre was killed, burnt to death. I – well you can see what happened to me.'

He wanted to turn to her as a sympathiser, to murmur polite words. If there had been a flicker of self-pity in her voice, perhaps he could have done. But her voice had been matter-of-fact as it told of the accident. As if it was something quite detached, something not quite credible that had happened to another person, to the memory of which she had long ago adapted herself. And suddenly he realised, fascinatedly, that for her there was no cripple, that she was – had willed herself to be – still the sun-kissed girl wandering through green French woodlands and gold-eared cornfields. Impressed as her half-wasted body was into the immovable pattern of the couch, yet it was still body that danced in the afternoon heat, until it was captured, tumbling into the cool water's embrace as into a lover's embrace ... What was she saying?

'Life was good. Rich. Full of warmth.'

And how was she looking? He dared not raise his eyes.

'To be in love. To be desired and to desire ...' Her voice was suddenly deep and strong, challenging. 'To be possessed.'

What was this: delirium, madness? No, he knew somehow the words were for him, especially for him. And, queerly, he found himself accepting them hungrily, wanting only to hear more words, whispered like caresses in her low, husky voice.

'There is nothing else in the world so unbearably sweet as being possessed, belonging to another's life.'

Now he must look. Some force stronger than himself was impelling his head upwards, raising his whole trembling body, commanding him to look at the woman on the couch.

And there she was, indeed. But now she was like a being afire, the light burning out of her eyes and sparkling off her hair, irradiating from the bare curves of her arms, spitting out of her parted mouth through the tiny red tip of her tongue. The fire convulsed her body and out of the flames he imagined it arising new and refreshed – surely it was the body of the girl dancing through the fields? At this new thought he banished the last shadow of his reasoning, his credulity, and meeting her gaze he lost himself, a diver into deep and unfathomable waters, into the huge, the enormous world that was her two devouring eyes.

'My God!' he whispered. 'Why didn't I see ... You're lovely ... You're alive ...'

'Pierre used to stroke my hair,' she said softly, and with a swift movement she put a hand behind her head and threw the mass of red hair forward like an offering.

'Oh!' he cried, and his hands awoke into action and plunged themselves in the hair.

'Oh, I want ... to be ... I am ... yours.'

And he buried his face in the hair, too, smelling its fragrance, while he moved his fingers round and round, caressingly. Very slowly – almost as if he were obeying a wish – he parted the hair and pushed it away until he was facing her, until her face and her lips and her eyes were so close as almost to be touching his own. Then he kissed her gently, as if in a dream.

That was how it happened. In the kiss, and in the gentle, erotic caresses that followed, he felt the deepest secrets of his being welling up and flowing across the physical contact and into her possession; so that, indeed, though there could be no physical consummation to their strange union, yet he was as sure as the day followed the night that in some inscrutable sense he had become possessed by her. It was eerie, sinister perhaps, but irresistible. It was as if she had physically re-created herself and her passion into the part of her that remained alive, and now, with her eyes and her hair and her hungry mouth and her soft, silky breasts, she loved and demanded his love with a power that overwhelmed him. At first, in moments of frantic detachment, he contemplated with horror the ultimate aridness and frustration of it. But he found it impossible to remain detached for long. And if he did she began telling him of her earlier life, in that same husky suggestive voice, and as the sound swept into him and bore away all his defences he found himself eager only to yield himself up to the fantastic power she had assumed over him.

So it became his whole life and purpose. His writing and his eating and his sleeping and his living were no longer for him or of him, but for her and of her. As she absorbed and devoured his strength and life of another, the woman Miriam seemed to grow and bloom and blossom like a radiant flower. But the man Edwards grew pale and thin, his eyes vacant and his face covered with strained lines, and his footsteps as he went about the house were unsure so that the other boarders began to look at him queerly and murmur to themselves. Now and then he was conscious of a dull pain in his heart, a vague sense of wistfulness, as of a man who had taken a wrong turning. But soon that feeling died, like many others.

For now he was possessed by a cripple woman with living eyes and a dead body, incorporated into the static functional pattern of a front sitting room world ... It would be a doubtful blessing that he was unlikely to endure as efficiently as the steel post, the rope pulley, or even the wooden candlesticks.

XII

A Rose In Winter

The girl made no great impression at first. She came up the manor drive wearing a drab black overcoat and a faded white scarf that almost entirely covered her fair hair. The face seemed pale and subdued, the eyes fixed resolutely on the gravel drive ahead, and indeed the girl walked and held herself with a curious diffidence as if anxious to keep herself withdrawn from too much attention. Only the legs, gleaming white against the dark background, conveyed a suggestion of life. Watching from the sitting room window Mrs Simmonds, the housekeeper, reflected with satisfaction upon the burdens she could pass on to this mouselike creature. Yet, watching from the door of the greenhouse, the young gardener saw only the legs, their easy, generous swelling, and knew at once in his instinctive way that there was experience in their walk. He licked his lips and rubbed his thick fingers up and down the smoothed wood of his spade handle, feeling sleepy fires stirring within him.

At the door, Mrs Simmonds eyed the girl carefully before admitting her into the wealth and luxury of the great hall, with its Persian carpets and antique furnishings, and the great glittering glass chandelier poised over the marble centre piece.

'You're the maid from the agency?'

'Yes.'

'I'm the housekeeper here. I'll show you to your room. You'll find a uniform on the bed. When you're ready come down to the kitchen and I'll explain your duties.'

The room was hardly more than an attic, a poky rather uncomfortable little place tucked right up in the gables and reached only by a rickety back stairway which began down in one of the pantries. Even Mrs Simmonds exhibited signs of uncomfortableness as she opened the door upon the room's bareness, the iron bedstead, the mahogany washstand, the dresser, the small table and chair, all outlined rather crudely against the faded floral-pattern wallpaper.

But the girl did not seem to mind. And when the housekeeper had gone she stood in the centre of the room looking around her with a curious warmth in her eyes; as if she was satisfied enough to be in a room of her own, as if this small, tucked-away box might in fact well suit her unobtrusive desires.

After a while the girl crossed to the dresser and looked into the tall, narrow mirror. There was a crack across the top so that the girl saw herself in two parts – the face pale and familiar above the crack, the rest of her, anonymously hidden behind black folds of cloth, below the crack. There was something that rather fascinated her about this conception, and for a long time she stared into the mirror, wondering about all sorts of things that had happened to the distorted familiar figure before her.

Then the girl began to undress. She took off her overcoat and threw it over the bedrail, and unbuttoned her blouse. And now a strange thing happened. As she began to divest herself of her clothes, and her body became gradually revealed, so the girl's personality seemed to undergo a subtle change. Where there had been soberness and anonymity, now there shone from the white flesh a sudden force and power, an impulse of harsh energy that could be felt as much as seen. The girl herself seemed aware of it: she hesitated before at last undoing her brassiere, and then with a curious movement of unwilling pleasure she stripped off her last garments and stood naked before the mirror. At once the impression of change was vividly confirmed. The girl's face now grew animated: with the removal of the scarf her long fair hair tumbled and flowed over her shoulders, and her eyes shone brightly as they stared into the mirror. Far from being drab and dull she was suddenly vibrant with life, a vibrancy that filled the air of the room, something strange and erotic that exuded from the girl's exposed figure. It was a thick-set rather slim body, so that each curve and hollow seemed emphasised, almost grossly so. The effect was this sense of power, so that when, as now, the girl gently cupped her breasts in her hands and looked down at their blue-veined shapes wonderingly, an impression of feeling and movement seemed to emerge from the breasts themselves, as if they quivered and sought fulfilment.

Slowly the girl ran her hands down her body, following the thick curves and swells with reflective familiarity. As she did so her lips parted slightly and exposed her teeth in what seemed, in the mirror, a smile. Yet somehow it was not a smile, but rather something furtive and animal-like, almost bestial; a look full of twisted sadistic memories from which, ultimately, the girl herself recoiled, as if in loathing. But it was some moments before that recoil; and in the interval the girl stared as if in fascination at what she saw as if she were seeing her body experiencing all that it had experienced, hating and loathing what she saw and yet unable to resist giving herself up to the contemplation. When at last she forced her gaze away from the mirror, she trembled all over; her breast heaved violently, and a look of despair dulled and faded her eyes.

At last, the paroxysm eased and passed, and with a long sigh, the girl seemed to return to reality. Her eyes fell upon the maid's black uniform spread neatly on the bed, and she held it up for inspection. There was something heavy and staid, almost ugly, about the uniform, but the girl did not seem to mind at all. Without looking again at the mirror she dressed again and pulled the uniform over her head until it hung around her body in heavy folds. At once the girl faded into her original personality. With deft movements she wound her long hair up into an inoffensive bun, pinned into shape with the maid's starch cap on top. When finally, she looked in the mirror again, there was not an inch of her body to be seen. Even her legs were resolutely encased in thick black stockings. It was not a pretty or exciting sight, but the girl seemed to find it pleasing. Or rather, perhaps it was that she felt safer. Thick-cloaked anonymity gave her protection from herself – the self that had gleamed and shone like hard polished stone from the mirror, and of which she was mortally afraid.

Mrs Simmonds was not altogether sure about the new maid. There was, she felt, something a little too secretive in her manner. This very secrecy left the housekeeper curiously uncertain of her authority. To reassure herself she kept the maid hard at work, cleaning and sweeping and dusting and performing a host of often unnecessary menial tasks. Almost the only compensation was that such a variety of work took the girl all over the vast, echoing house. It was one of the old manor houses, built in the Elizabethan age of grandeur and cultured tastes, and still retaining much evidence and atmosphere of those bygone days. Moving from one great room to another, pausing to marvel at some rich and colourful tapestry, some intricate wood carving or a canvas alive with the portrait of some smiling cavalier of the past, the maid became interested despite herself. She could not help contrasting the generosity of space, the wealth of colour and comfort, with the tight confinements of the suburban house where she had previously worked. She found, as she moved about dusting and cleaning the rooms ready for the twice weekly occasion when they were thrown open for visits to the public, that she experienced a real pleasure in her journeys. Sometimes she would even pause and stand back and half imagine the rooms alive again with past ages – or, looking out over the grounds, she might pretend to spy some great cortage of knights and their ladies approaching up the winding driveway.

One afternoon, standing by a great bay window where the sunshine streamed through tiny panelets and surrounded her with light, the maid suddenly became aware of a second presence in the room. He was tall and broad shouldered, grey-haired and with a keen but heavily lined face on which now there showed an expression of surprise. He advanced forward slowly, his eyes fixed with curious penetration upon the girl, so that she stood where she was, silhouetted against the light.

'Who are you?'

The girl flushed.

'I'm the new maid, sir.'

'Oh, yes. Of course.' The man's face cleared somewhat, as if for a moment he had been thinking of something else. Now he smiled politely, and the girl found herself responding to the sudden warmth that exuded from what, to her, seemed quite an old man. She, too, smiled, and took a step forward. As she did so, her whole body seemed to break into movement and light, and the life in her rose up and was revealed, fresh and young, despite all the shadowiness of her drab uniform. Even Methuselah would have responded, and this man, though old, was by no means as old as that. His eyes gleamed beneath their bushy eyebrows and he looked at the girl with fresh interest.

'And where d'you come from?'

'From the agency, sir.'

'No, no – I mean your home, girl.'

The maid hesitated, and the man eyed her reflectively. He had soft, almost grey eyes that half the time seemed to be looking far away into the distance. Perhaps it was this that accounted for an impression he gave of not being wholly present: as if his physical body, solid in sturdy tweed, was there in the room, but his personality was diffused, escaped elsewhere. Yet his eyes missed nothing.

'I have no home, sir.'

The man nodded, as if he had expected the remark.

'You have that look about you. I'm sorry... I hope – ' He paused, as if thinking better of his words. Instead, he waved a hand round the room. 'What do you think of all this?'

'I like it, sir.' And then, as if feeling the words inadequate, the maid repeated: 'I like it very much, sir.'

'Good,' said the man. 'There's much beauty in the world you know – what's your name?'

'Gillian, sir.'

'Well, Gillian, you'll find plenty of beautiful things here. Appreciate them while you can. One day, when there's time, I'll show you round and explain things properly.'

'Thank you, sir.'
'Don't mention it.'
With a friendly nod he turned and went out of the room, leaving the girl staring after him curiously.

Later, back in the kitchen, she recounted the experience to Mrs Simmonds.

'Who was he?'

'Why, Sir Gerald, of course.' Mrs Simmonds looked self-important. 'He's the owner of this place. At least, he used to be. It really belongs to the National Trust now, you know. One of the stately homes of England idea ... But Sir Gerald still lives here. He's a widower, you know. Wife died about ten years ago.'

'What was she like?' said the maid, with a stir of interest.

Mrs Simmonds reflected.

'Well, she was a very lovely woman, very lovely indeed. Rather too much aware of the fact, in my opinion. Always dressed up to kill, so to speak. And even at home – my word, she used to fair shock me sometimes, wandering about half-naked ...'

'Why shouldn't she, if it was her home?' The maid felt a sudden sympathy with the dead woman, thinking secretly how if it was her house she would have liked to do that, to feel it an intimate, secret world belonging to her, wherein she could be completely natural.

Mrs Simmonds pursed her lips, to reflect her disapproval not only of the late lady of the house, but of the younger generation of maids.

'That's a matter of opinion, my girl ... However, the poor thing's gone now, rest her soul.'

'And were they happy?'

'Yes,' said Mrs Simmonds grudgingly. 'I must admit they always struck me as a very happy couple.'

For some reason her words remained with the maid, and as she went about her duties that day she found herself thinking about this past era, imagining the grey-haired man and his lovely wife in their life together. Such a life had always seemed remote and unreal to her, but now she existed in the very atmosphere she felt she could almost imagine the two of them together. And in her mind the grey-haired man took on a new resilience; she saw him as he was perhaps ten or twenty years ago, the body springy, the lines faded from the face, which was quite handsome, with strong boned features, and thick dark hair.

The girl found a curious pleasure in contemplating this detached vision. It was rather like looking into a quiet pool and watching images reflected there. There was a peacefulness and a serenity about such contemplation which was new to the girl. It was new because she was using a new faculty, a mind. Always in the past she had experienced sensations through her body only; indeed it had hardly occurred to her that it could be otherwise. But now, moving about this great house with its echoes of past wonders, she found herself experiencing sensations with her mind – just as she found herself thinking of the house's owner with her mind, seeing him as a man, yes, but mostly as a being, a personality, whose existence, unknown until that day, already gave her a curious sense of comfort, of added safety.

In the evening the girl had some free time, so she decided to take a walk through the long bottom woods that led eventually down to a curling river. It was a lovely Spring evening, with the fading sunlight falling softly on green leaves and shrubs. Walking along the soft woodland paths was like walking through some fairy land: birds chattering in the beech trees leant a nostalgic background of music. The girl felt a sense of wonder, apprehending the magical quality of existence itself.

Coming round a bend she saw a small clearing ahead of her. Sitting on a fallen tree, whittling with a knife at a small branch, was the young gardener.

The girl approached warily, conscious at once of the gardener's physical presence. Aware of her awareness, he went on carving at the piece of wood, his thick brown forearms gleaming in the sunlight. Only when the girl was almost level did he look up, and then it was a sharp, almost cruel glance, before which the girl was helpless. She knew, instinctively, that he was seeing her right through the pitiful protection of her dark uniform, seeing her as she really was, the white flesh exposed and revealed, shaped by the touches of many men, their desires, their practices. She felt suddenly sickened: and yet, despite herself, she received and sensually nurtured the gardener's hot glance.

'Taking a walk, Gillian?'

'Maybe.'

'Mind if I come?'

She shrugged.

'Please yourself.'

She resumed walking, and the gardener fell into stride beside her, swinging his limbs loosely as he walked. She saw that he still carried the piece of wood, and sensing her interest, he held it up. She saw that his knife had hacked great savage jagged shapes into the wood, but as yet there was no completion to the shape.

'What are you making?' she asked.

He smiled, a swift movement that lit up his young face and gave it an added attraction. She could feel all the power and strength and confidence of his youthfulness exuding from him – a power that was at once frightening and attractive. As if divining her thoughts, he took the wood and flung it far away into the undergrowth.

'It's not important.'

They walked along together in silence. For a few moments she tried to think of something to say: then, suddenly, she realised that there was no place for conversation, that the man beside her was concentrating all his thoughts, all his will, all the power within him, upon compelling her to him. The physical force of his will was so intense that for a moment the girl was almost rooted to where she stood. At the same moment, the old conflict broke within her. With a sudden cry, not so much of fear as of helplessness, she ran blindly down the path.

Behind her she heard the gardener give a shout. Then he called again, and she knew from the tone that he took it all for a game. She could imagine his great body breaking into a run after her. He would run after her leisurely, teasingly, always within reach, but perhaps letting her run on and on. At last, confidently, he would catch up with her, she would feel his hand upon her shoulder, gripping tight, angrily, urgently.

The girl cried out, not at the moment, but at the memory of all the past times. The chase in the city streets, the chase in the crowded shop, the chase in every corner of existence; the familiar hot glance that she could never avoid, that kindled some wayward bitter fire within herself. The great waves of desire beating upon her like the sea upon the shore, waves that would reach on and on until she was submerged beneath them. And yet she could never drown; that was perhaps the most awful thing. She could never drown and melt into the nothingness that everyone else seemed to achieve.

The path ahead broke open into the sudden sunshine of a field; beyond lay the cool glittering waters of the river. Ahead was a sense of peace, of quietude, which she had never known.

Blindly, with a cry of hopelessness, the girl turned off the path, and plunged heavily into the tangled undergrowth. She brushed her way past several trees and clumps of bushes, until she had plunged down a slope and into a shadowy clearing. There she threw herself on to the ground and waited, her body half crouching as if already she was some animal of the jungle.

The gardener easily found her there. Looking down, a little smile playing at his mouth, he felt no doubts, no pity, no compunction. He saw only the quarry, himself the hunter: there, spread-eagled against the soft bed of last year's leaves, the conquest. Lithely he bent down and reached his arm out to touch the girl's shoulder. Feeling the strange throbbing vitality beneath the black costume, he pulled her round to face him. Looking up into his face the girl saw not one but many faces; they swam before her in a helpless, hopeless circle, one face and another, merging and emerging, until she was no longer clear whose face was which. The sea swept over her, that was enough. Caught up in the physical moment, she hissed and spat, clawed and caressed, fought – and yielded. The conflict was always there, never ceased. And when all was over and the man lay back sleepily, the girl could not find sleep. She lay staring up yearningly towards the blue sky, an infinite distance away, and there seemed to her an inevitability about the way in which the tall tree branches closed and then opened, so that no sooner did she see the sky than the vision was obliterated again.

For a few days the maid tried to avoid the gardener. It was an impossible aim, for his presence always hovered about her. Walking across the drive she would be conscious of him watching her from where he worked on one of the great circular flower beds. Sitting on the kitchen steps, peeling potatoes in the sunlight, she would look up and see his dark face at the window of the stable loft that was his home. Always she hesitated to meet his eyes, for they were like mirrors that reflected her own secrets. He knew her as Mrs Simmonds and the normal outside world could not know her, that slumbering sensual part of her that she had cloaked in vain, beneath drab black clothes. He had the instinctive animal cunning that could arouse her body to passion and desire. But he had not the intelligence to appreciate the conflict in her, to taste the dust in her mouth of surrender.

In the daytime the maid immersed herself in the activities of the house. At night the hours hung more heavily, more emptily. Sitting reading the newspaper at the kitchen table while Mrs Simmonds sewed by the fire, she would look out of the window and see the bright light above the stable, and its glittering eye seemed to beckon her into fire and oblivion. She remembered days of childhood, the inevitable attraction of a side street leading away into escape, into other worlds – and how often she had darted away, with a taunt and a laugh, to wander into a maze of streets and people. She had never been able to resist the temptation, yet she had never reached a destination, never found the person for whom she secretly looked.

And so now, as if by habit, she could never resist getting up and putting on her coat and slipping out quietly into the night. Sometimes she simply wanted to escape into the dark, to walk for mile after mile along the quiet country lanes within whose oblivion she felt at ease. And yet, even then, even as she vanished down the lane, she would see that burning light in the stable loft extinguished; she would know that he was aware of her departure, was descending into the night to haunt her with his presence. At this, the anger would burn in her and she would run blindly into the dark, on and on and down little turnings and footpaths until she was sure she was alone, and escaped from her problem. Yet always, mysteriously, magically, he would appear, a shadow in the darkness, a rough voice whispering, 'Taking a walk, Gillian?'

In the dark, at least, it became illicit and exciting; an undercurrent of mystery and fearful expectation took possession of her. At his final touch she made no struggle, responding with an angry despair his embraces – matching desire for desire, lust for lust. And in the dark, somehow, the shadowiness swallowed up all else, perhaps she came nearer to reaching oblivion than anywhere else. In her imagination he became not so much a particular man, or even men, but the night itself, sinewy arms of darkness taking her into their embrace of death.

But one night he persuaded her to climb up to the stable loft, up the long wooden ladder and into the big, hollow sort of room that seemed cut off from the whole world. By the light of a paraffin lamp she saw that the room was hardly furnished at all. There was a table and chairs, some sort of cupboard, and a small palliasse bed, no more. This did not worry her; but the flickering light did. Its constancy, its certitude, fretted her. It was like some unwelcome revelation of the sparsity of her life.

'Put out the light ... put it out!' she whispered.

But the man would not do it. She knew that he wanted to watch her, to see her face, to taunt and tantalise her before his eyes. She was suddenly filled with disgust, with repugnance, when he picked her up and lay her upon the small bed that reeked with the sweat and smell of his body, his work – she sprang to her feet with an exclamation of horror. She knew from the fatuous, mocking smile with which he greeted her cry, that it meant nothing to him. He was not aware of her with his mind, only with his body. And something of this thought remained with her throughout that evening, neutralising all desire, all passion, leaving her as cold and beyond his reach as the table and chairs, the high beams of the rafters. That night, for the first time, he was baffled and disappointed with her; but she, for her part, realised that she had never been with him, that he had never reached her. The fearful thought hung around her, that no one could, no one would.

After a fortnight, Mrs Simmonds suggested that the maid might now take over the task of preparing and taking up Sir Gerald's breakfast, which he always had in bed.

'He likes his tea strong, brown sugar, cream ... four slices of toast and a boiled egg ... and a bowl of fruit. Eight o'clock sharp.'

The maid was glad of the new duty. Unlike the elder woman she was not bothered by rising early. She quite enjoyed the preparation of this solitary breakfast, coming down and raking out the fire and boiling up the kettle and water for the egg. When she filled the bowl with fruit she carefully selected two round and juicy looking oranges, some nice rosy red apples, and a large soft pear that looked as if it would melt in the mouth.

At eight o'clock sharp she knocked quietly on the massive oak doorway of Sir Gerald's first floor room. After getting no answer to a further knock she opened the door and went in quietly. Putting the tray down on a table, she walked over to the huge windows and drew back the thick blue curtains, flooding the room with bright sunshine. She looked around curiously at the tapestries and period furniture, the Chippendale chairs and dresser, the gold lined otterman, the Adam fireplace, and in one corner the great double poster bed still carrying along its top the rich gold and red frieze embossed with a coat of arms.

In the centre of the bed, curled up under the bedclothes in an attitude of relaxation, of complete peace, lay her employer. It struck the girl how naturally he belonged – to the bed, to the room, to the whole period of past elegance. She had the feeling that perhaps he had lain there, like that, at peace with the world, not just for the night, but for years, perhaps for a hundred years. There was that impression of permanency about the grey-haired sleeping man.

And yet, tip-toeing nearer to satisfy her curiosity, she was surprised to see how strangely young he looked – how, in sleep, the lines of his face seemed smoothed away as if in dreams he became again the young, the attractive man he must have been (though to the girl it was not this aspect, this past attractiveness, that interested, but the present impression of strength, of authority, of understanding). Even as he slept there, perhaps a thousand miles away from her in his thoughts, she was yet conscious of comfort in his presence.

As she bent forward, staring thoughtfully, Sir Gerald stirred, turned on to his back, and suddenly opened his eyes wide. What always mystified the maid afterwards, what she never quite understood, was how immediately he recognised her, how quickly he smiled; how simply he drew her into the intimacy of his life. She forgot that he encountered her in a moment of honesty, that though she might have called it curiosity she was nevertheless advancing to meet him even as he awoke to her presence.

'Ah, Gillian, so you've brought the breakfast. Good. Mrs Simmonds didn't mind?'

'No, sir,' she replied, and she knew by the way he said it that it was he who had instructed the housekeeper to make the change.

She picked the tray off the table and brought it over to the bed, waiting a moment or two while he sat up and smoothed out the bedclothes before gently putting it on his knees.

'Ah! Tea with cream ... crisp toast, and a fresh egg. A nice way to start the day, don't you think?'

She smiled without answering, and then gently touched the bowl of fruit, as if proffering it to him. At the gesture he looked at her warmly, a smile hovering at his lips. Some further impulse made her pick the single pear, and offer it to him. He showed no surprise, but took the pear from her, his warm fingers brushing hers with the lightest of touches ... and she noted, in a fleeting but memorable moment, that he held the pear exactly as she had given it to him, and seemed deliberately to bite into the part she had held.

It was a small, almost trivial, yet so intimate a thing that the maid felt herself completely at a loss. She did not know now what to say, what to do, or where to look. All she knew was a desire to remain. If he had told her, conventionally, that she could now go, a blackness and despair such as she had never before experienced would have fallen upon her. That she knew instinctively; but beyond that, she was bewildered and lost.

He came to her rescue gently, tactfully.

'Won't you sit down a minute, Gillian? I don't particularly like breakfasting on my own. Mrs Simmonds is such a garrulous old lady that I can never bring myself to invite her company. But you, my dear, you look as if you would make a good listener.'

And so, she felt, she could be. For his voice had a strange, musical resonance, as if his words, like him, were steeped in age and experience. She felt she could sit there and listen for hours to his voice, running on, gently and smoothly, like the flow of a river. For she knew, by her instincts, that he had things to say and tell her that were necessary in her life.

Yet, with all that, and almost without her knowledge, it was he who listened, she who talked.

At first she talked haltingly, nervously. Then, suddenly, as if something was released in her, she spoke without cease, without restraint. She spoke of a strange, alien, faraway world from which she had sprung, like grass in a wilderness.

Cardiff, by the docks. Where her aunt had kept a cafe, one of those small, dingy places full of seamen and hangers on, all kinds and colours, little Chinamen and huge lost looking negroes with mournful faces. A world of dim lights, the dark night, a perpetual furtiveness. Here her aunt had reigned supreme, a pretty buxom woman, dressed up in tight blonde hair and a rich red mouth, and legs that the sailors used to stare at unblinkingly. Her aunt didn't need to run the cafe, for her husband had a job as second engineer on a ship, and sent her good money. But the truth was she needed the glitter and glamour, the admiration, and – the men, too. She needed them clustering around her like flies around a bright light; needed their admiration, their desire, their longing, their conquests.

'But your parents, your father and mother?'

The girl wouldn't talk about them. And, listening, the older man understood that they might as well never have existed, that they had been shadows passing by – two nebulous people who had simply brought her into existence and left her to fend for herself. It was the aunt, the cafe, the faded lights, the staring men, the undercurrent of crude desire, of animal wants – these things that had created the girl. Upon such foundations she had flowered, growing to girlhood, aware suddenly of the men's stares swivelling from her aunt to herself, looking not at her aunt's silk stockings, but at her own bare, brown legs, with their gentle swell of youth.

'They all had the same way of looking. A sort of hungry look. Made me feel quite ill sometimes ... and then again, you know, I used to rather like it. Gave me a feeling of power. I used to play them up, like my aunt did. Used to give them a look back, bold as brass. Come-to-bed look, one of them said it was.' The girl gave a short laugh. 'Well, of course, when my aunt tumbled to what was happening she got proper mad. Went for me one day, screaming and shouting, hitting me on the head, real fury she was in. 'Cos she was twice my age, you see, and the men couldn't help noticing, I 'spose. I ought to have felt sorry for her, I 'spose. But I was too frightened. She hit me and scratched me and told me to get out ... and so I got out. On the streets, I was, with nowhere to go.'

And as the girl's voice slackened, approaching the painful memory, the man's imagination took up her story from her. He became the girl herself, alone among the streets, the dark alleys, the tall tenement houses; alone in the jungle, where a thousand pitiless eyes watched. And always pursued ... by shadows in the night, by men never really known, by that eternal hungry look. It was something the man could only comprehend by imagination, and he guessed that the reality may have been beyond imagination.

'You didn't go back to your aunt, then?'

'No,' said the maid. 'No, never.'

Somehow the way she said the last word stirred Sir Gerald's pity.

'Never is a big word,' he said. 'Let's leave it alone for a while. It doesn't always do to look back too much. My goodness, I'm glad I don't have to do it very often. Think of all the years ...'

'But you're not all that old,' said the maid. And then, as if coming back to the present, she added: 'sir.'

'Old enough to be your father!' – the reply was on the tip of his tongue, but he checked himself in time, smiling at her with his warm grey eyes that filled her with such assurance, such trust.

'Well, Gillian, take away the breakfast things now and I'll get up and have a bath.'

She nodded and picked up the tray and walked over to the door. As she was going out, she caught a glimpse of him swinging out of the bed and donning a dressing gown for the journey to the bathroom. She thought vaguely of that tall figure standing under the shower, water cascading down and swishing away all the years of fatigue. And her curious contemplation of Sir Gerald, standing clean and brown and straight, was the first time she had ever thought of a man in that way, from the heart.

Later he took her on his promised tour of the house. It was a grey, forbidding day outside, but in these great rooms there was constant colour and warmth, that took on new radiance under the skilful touch of his voice. He had a simple, direct way of talking about things that encouraged her understanding. Some of the things that he told her were beyond her, but the rest seeped steadily into her consciousness. She began to understand the reality of such things as tradition, of culture, of art, of grace – above all, of grace.

'Grace is everything in all things. Whatever we do or aspire towards, we should fulfil with grace and understanding. Not to do so, to rush at things, to smash our way through life, is to miss the beauty of life.'

And he tried to teach her something of the beauties that surround life – paintings, tapestries, music, poetry – so that she might come to realise, perhaps in her own time and of her own volition, that there was meant to be a beauty in life itself, in the way it was lived. Leisure for haste, dignity for crudity, savouring for savagery – these were some of the alternatives he tried to bring before her mind, so that she might begin to understand the complexity of life, and so of herself.

When the tour was finished, the girl's mind was in a jumble and a muddle. She spent the evening thinking about the things he had said, the things she had seen; contemplating in marvel the great mystery of life. That night her sleep was populated with strange dreams and images. She felt lost and a little frightened, and was glad when the sunshine falling through the skylight awoke her to a new day, her new task. Taking in his breakfast, she felt at once familiar and yet curiously shy.

He was ready for her this morning, his grey eyes watching with evident appreciation.

'You don't mind my talking like this?' she asked nervously.

'No. Far from minding, I want you to.' And he got out of bed and walked over to one of the bay windows, as if it was easier for him to talk looking out upon the beloved, familiar landscape.

'You've never talked like this to anyone, have you?'

'No, sir.' The girl's voice was a whisper in the great room. 'It's a great help to me, to be able to talk to someone.'

Sir Gerald turned round. His face was set, almost stern: the lines engraved suggested only wisdom, not age, to the watching girl. When he smiled, there was something lovely and brave that shone out of the face.

'My dear, perhaps we can help one another – has that not occurred to you? I think you must be one of the most lonely and unloved people I have ever met, but I know of another such person.' He paused, and then lied gently: 'I mean, of course, myself ... Perhaps I need you, Gillian, just as much as perhaps you need someone like me.'

He beckoned the girl to come and sit down in the chair

beside him. As she did so, he undid the maid's cap, and began running his fingers through her hair with a gentle movement that she found very restful.

'Now, my dear, talk away. Tell me the rest, the parts you never finished yesterday.'

Then she told him. About the men, the ones with the hungry look that had never let her alone, that had followed her like ferrets down to the last hiding place, before whose relentless pursuit she became helpless and vanquished. And as she talked her face became consumed in the old bestial look of the animal, so that the watching man felt the ache of pity in his heart for her, who had never known love, but only lust. But he said nothing, just listened, as the girl told him about one man after another, lovers creeping upon her in the night, so many names and faces that the imagination boggled to think that a human being could endure so much.

'But,' said the girl doggedly, and he loved her for being honest, 'It cannot only have been their fault. It was something to do with me, too. I – I even began to want it, in some sort of way. I mean, you know ...'

'I know,' he said gently. 'To be touched, to be caressed, to feel the winds of desire blowing about your body, making it alive – my dear, that is only natural. There's nothing wrong with that, it is what all lovers want, and feel. But there must be something else with it, mustn't there? We must care, we must love – without love, it is a mockery.'

'Ah,' said the girl, 'That I know.' And she looked up and stared at Sir Gerald with eyes as blank and hard as beach pebbles, until he could bear the sight no longer, and bent forward gently and kissed those poor young eyes that had seen so much, and yet so little.

'Why did you do that?' said the girl in a whisper.

'Because I wanted to.'

'Kiss my eyes again,' said the girl. 'Kiss them again.' And he knew she had never said that before, not to anyone, and his heart ached again.

But as he bent forward and kissed her eyes again, a change came over him, too, and he realised how little we any of us know ourselves. For he felt old, forgotten fires stirring within him; at the touch of his lips upon her soft flesh, he felt the flame run through him as if it had been flung out of the far heavens. I've not felt that for years, he thought ruefully. And he was glad to be born again.

He was gentle with her, though, and incredibly patient. He sent her away then, and he did not kiss her again until the next day. And then it was the same almost wistful kiss, a fragrant and light thing that touched her hair, her cheeks, her eyes, her soft hair – but not yet her lips, stirring with familiar hunger.

She was puzzled, and yet strangely at ease. She supposed it was because he was old that he did not respond as ardently, as savagely, as brutally as the men who followed her with their eyes, as the young gardener who watched her and consumed her for his own vanity. And yet the passivity was not displeasing: it lapped around her like gentle waters, and she basked in its placidity and peace, while yet conscious of a tingle of excitement at what might yet be. It was the first time she had not been possessed and obliterated: her reaction to his gentle tolerance, his quiet observation of her own individuality, was an instinctive turning towards him. She was filled with that ever recurring desire to know more about him, about his life; the things that had made him as he was, that had given him that curious serenity.

But when she asked he laughed, dismissing in a gesture his own lifetime.

'It is not important, Gillian. The moment only is important.'

And he took her arm and led her up the huge staircase, up much higher than his own room, right to the very top of the front part of the house. Here, through a green doorway, he ushered her into a huge studio room, as long as three of the ordinary rooms. It's polished floor was covered at intervals with thick rugs and straw mats, but there was no furniture in the room except the window seats.

It was the first time the maid had seen the room. She stood looking round her in wonder, sensing the room's significance, its memories.

'My wife used this room as a studio,' explained Sir Gerald.

'She was a painter. Quite a good one.'

The maid looked round.

'Can I see some?'

He eyed her gravely.

'No, my dear. Before she died she asked that they all be destroyed.' He hesitated. 'You see, Gillian, my wife and I shared not only our bodies and our interests, but even our beliefs. We both believed, as I said just now, in the moment. We believed, and we tried to act on that belief, that every moment is the most wonderful moment in the world – that we should capture the last ounce of happiness and fulfilment from each possible moment.'

'I know,' said the maid. 'Gather rosebuds while ye may ... there a song.'

Sir Gerald's eyes twinkled.

'I'd like to hear you sing that, Gillian.'

'Would you?' She looked at him shyly, but anxious to please. She sang in a low, rather sweet voice:

'Gather rosebuds while ye may ...'

The sound of the voice seemed to fill the room with strange echoes, or so the older man thought. And his grey eyes, searching round the room, perhaps saw other sights than the emptiness, the carpets, the lovely divan.

When Gillian finished the song, he was standing close beside her, one arm resting on her shoulder. At its touch she felt the deep warmth of him seeping into her in ebb and flow, like the summer tide. Not wanting to disturb the sweetness of the moment, she stood absolutely still.

And he, beside her, savoured her youth, her hope, her freshness; that at his touch, miraculously, seemed to be born again, in a way virginal.

When he slowly turned her round to face him, there were tears in his eyes.

'Why,' said the girl, 'You're crying ...'.

And, wonderingly, she put up her fingers to brush away the tears, rubbing her finger tips slowly up the lines of his cheek and sweeping each tear away with a slow gesture of finality.

'You mustn't cry ...'

And now all sorts of strange and new sensations flooded into the girl's being, gathered in her breast in great knots that swelled and struggled to burst – until she wanted to cry out with the pain of it, and the agony of her mind was revealed on her young face.

At the sight of it, he pulled her close to him, and put his arms around her in a long embrace of finality.

'My dear,' he whispered, as he felt age-old feelings welling up in him that he thought had died. He trembled within himself before the surge of his protective, anxious caring for this child.

'My dear ...'

And for her, his voice was like music, his arms like a blessing, his warmth like a benediction. She could not speak, for the words were lacking. But she felt in every limb, in her bones, in her blood, this surge of new feeling, new hope, new fulfilment.

'Ah,' she said, her lips moist, her eyes wet. 'Ah ... Ah ...' And then she looked at him fearfully.

'Why,' whispered the maid, 'I feel ... I feel ...' and the other words stumbled out awkwardly, '... for you.'

He carried her in his arms then to the divan, depositing her gently upon the gold braided cover. Then he lay beside her, curling his body gently around hers to give her warmth. His hands, soft and delicate, touched her breasts and fondled them gently. At their touch she felt the circle complete, felt enclosed within the circle of his being.

They lay like that for nearly an hour, without stirring any more. For the girl it was a wonderful yet shocking experience, to be made aware of herself in that way, to receive more rich pleasure from the touch of an older man's wise hands on her breasts than from all the hot embraces of younger men. She wanted to tell him so, but somehow she felt there was no need; he who seemed so aware of all her needs and problems would know that, too.

At the end of the hour, he raised himself slightly and looked down upon her face, half buried in the dark snow of hair. She saw his grey eyes full upon her, for the first time, and she looked into them fearlessly, with joy, with pride.

'My dear,' he said humbly, 'If I can make you happy a little ... If I can bring you life, real life ...'

But her shining eyes gave him the answer, and confirmed the doubts in his heart, the doubts of a man who has travelled through the world about entering the life of one who is still perhaps on the threshold. For this one had been bruised and battered, like a broken petal, and he thought that if he could mend the break, he would die a happier man than if he had wasted away the lonely days of a selfish recluse.

And very gently, for the first time, he bent forward and kissed the maid full upon her rose-bud lips. A loving tender kiss, whose message flowed to the very innermost depths of her being – at whose touch she felt herself carried faraway from her past, caught up in some greater stream that was full of rich and wonderful things. This was the kiss that brought her love; and whether it was the kiss of lover or father, or perhaps both, did not really matter.

After that the room at the top of the house became their secret, their place of the heart. Somehow he did not think his wife would have minded, rather that she would have wished just this, that he should use his knowledge to bring happiness to someone, his love to warm their hearts.

And somehow the girl did not mind about the wife, the lingering memory of her – rather did she secretly welcome it as some form of strength. She thought of her as a friend, this unknown woman who in her time had given such great happiness to this man: and thinking thus the maid would feel humbled, conscious of her own debt, her own deep resolve to give some happiness to the one who had brought her all happiness.

When he finally made love to her, many days, indeed weeks later, the maid was a different girl, another person. Things in her that had grown stunted and rotten, had somehow withered away, or been cast away. She had learned from his patience, tenderness, understanding. When he let his gathered passion ride, telling her with his eyes and his movements the reality of his love, he was surprised not only at the intuitive understanding of her response, but at the gentleness that tinged her passion, the purity of her consummation.

'You might almost be a virgin,' he suggested humorously.

But she shook her head and put a finger on his lips.

'Now now,' she whispered, and her smile was secret and known only to him. 'Now I am a bride.'

Marriage was not a thing either of them contemplated. It never even occurred to the girl, though Sir Gerald did wonder at one time. But he sensed, correctly, that it would have been unnecessary, like a stamp on a pact already sealed. He believed, in fact, that she would have resented even what might seem an honour, for fear it marred the flow of their relationship. Besides he knew something else – he knew that he had not very much longer to live.

The maid stayed at the manor house nearly two years. During that time she was hardly aware of the existence of the outside world, of other people. She never spoke again to the gardener. Her whole being was given up to the man with the grey hair and wise eyes, in the autumn of his existence. She believed that he was the love of her life, and that there could be no life beyond.

But he knew different, for he was a wise man. He knew that he was nurturing the seed, and that others must smell the blossom and marvel at the buds and pick the beautiful flowers. And his wisdom and his greatness was in knowing this, and accepting it, and having no regrets.

When the illness which he had fought off for years took a final hold on him, he told the girl she must go away. At first she would not believe him. Then she was aghast, horrified.

'No, no, I can't ... I can't leave you ... You've made me live.'

He looked at her sadly, a little pale, already settling into the decay of his illness. But his smile was strong and clear, like winter sunshine.

'No, Gillian. I've shown you how to live, perhaps. But that's all.'

And he was adamant about her going, not only for her sake,

but partly for his own, for he knew that the business of dying was a serious one that needed all his concentration.

'You go to London for a while, my dear. I'll give you addresses of friends. There's much for you to see and do there. And work, too – if you want it. Oh, you've a whole world at your feet, my dear. It will be exciting, thrilling – challenging!'

And at his words she thought he might be speaking an epitaph on himself, his own attitude to life. Humbly she took his tired body in her arms and held him close to her so that he could hear the firm beat of her young heart against his head.

'Ah, but you have given me so much ... so much. I shall never forget.'

'No,' he said mildly, 'I don't suppose you will.'

She went on a November month morning, cold and clear. The sky was still misty, but the rising sun blazed promise of brightness to come. He said goodbye to her up in their room, quietly, without fuss. She clung to him for a moment as if she would never let go. Then, as he was about to protest, she released her hold and vanished silently – she had learned much from him about the delicacy of human relationships. He watched her come out of the front door and get into the waiting taxi. She looked neat and smooth, well-groomed: a woman. He smiled faintly and watched until the taxi had disappeared down the drive. Only then did he allow the tears to fall, slow and silent, an old man's rain.

She sat back into the oblivion of the taxi, alone with her thoughts, herself. She turned the handkerchief over and over in her fingers.

'Please God,' she whispered. 'Please God let him die easily and without suffering.'

Then the taxi carried her away to the train for London. And as his memorial she began to live.

XIII

The Man They'll Mourn In Vain

The sun was over to the west, hanging just above a far row of trees, when Royce opened the throttle and sent the sleek white monoplane roaring across the airfield on its first altitude test. He sat rigid in the cockpit, his hand taut and precise on the joystick, holding it down firmly while the sound of the engine rose to a fierce whine. The plane streaked across the wide tarmac path, heading straight for the squatting shapes of the hangars. Almost imperceptibly his fingers crooked round the stick, pulling it back slowly into the folds of his leather flying coat. With a faint jerk the thin nose lifted and the plane came off the ground in a long, steady climb. It skimmed fifty feet above the yawning hangars and rose into the sky like a triumphant sea-gull, the short tapering wings cutting through the air with a hissing crescendo of sound – the stream-lined bodywork glittering in the sunlight. Touching the throttle further forward he eased his left foot on the rudder-bar, bringing the plane round in a zooming curve. For a moment he leaned out of the cockpit, letting the fresh wind cut across his face, watching fascinatedly as the sharp shadow of the plane stabbed across the revolving grey-green blob of the airfield. Then he drew back, shutting the sliding roof of the cockpit, and straightened out the plane, pointing the nose up and away from home.

As he felt the effortless float of his body through the air he settled into his seat, aware of a warm, familiar sense of contentment stealing over him. It was the final escape, without which he would have been crushed under the burden of his public and private lives. Now he could almost forget the frantic overworking of the past few days, the long night vigil making sure everything was ready, the morning's fretful wait for permits from necessary officials and inspectors. These were infinitesimal items, belonging to the immovable earth, buried into the intricate patterns of human existence, successes and failures. They disappeared suddenly from his mind, along with the staccato list of older memories ... The air marshal shaking his head doubtfully. The aircraft inspector wagging a reprimanding finger. The departmental chief politely opening the door. The aeronautical correspondent shrugging his shoulders helplessly. The manufacturers of the superjet aero-engine telephoning their endless excuses for delays. Finding the money, finding the site, finding the materials, finding the men. Building, building, building, working, working, working: blueprints, schedules, models, layouts, superstructures: machine tools and machinery, skilled hands and skilled heads, rivets and wire struts and dope for the wings, paint for the fuselage and mercury for the altitude level. Spring and summer and autumn and winter and spring and summer and autumn and winter and spring and summer and autumn and winter and spring ... Hold-ups and bottlenecks, delays and shortages, draughts from waiting outside a hundred officials' doorways. Now, in a moment, the vast panorama of petty jealousies and obstacles appeared before his eyes – to be ripped swiftly into a thousand shreds by the whirling propeller. Let it all go, years and years of it, let them all rot. It was incredible but it was true. He was here in the plane, and around him all the wide waiting sky.

Here, airborne, himself and the plane welded into a smooth entity, life seemed miraculously lightened. The personal conflicts that, on earth, weighed like a heavy burden now melted into a sudden sea of peace and simplicity. There was a flow of lightness penetrating into his body, into the movement of his limbs, into the river of his blood – washing his whole being with cool, soothing waters. In that transient time he was conscious of being at the end of one journey and at the beginning of another. For a moment he gave himself up restfully to the gentle flow of thoughts and feelings. Then, mind crystal clear, he pulled out the sliding notebook with its chained pencil and began jotting down the facts of his trade.

> *Take off.* Normal but when tail comes up full left rudder is required.
> *Climbing.* With full service load climbs 4,000 feet in 2 minutes.
> *Lateral Control.* The ailerons are unusually powerful ...

In the whole time since he had pulled on the thick rubber boots and snapped the catch on his leather jerkin, standing in the mud while the mechanics tuned up the engine, his mind had been possessed completely by the plane and its purpose.

Along the low, bramble hedge lining the aerodrome's environs Mathilde sat silent at the wheel of the coupe, her hands white and uneasy as they gripped the wheel. She wore black, because he liked her best in black, and the colour merged indefinably into the darkness of the car so that her face and her hands stood out startlingly by their white comparison. There was a simple yet subtle elegance about her, a trimness and a polish that she fostered, again, because she knew it was how he liked her. He liked, he said, to be able to feel her shape with his hands as something known and familiar. And she liked him, also, to feel it as something beautiful – as beautiful as the white monoplane.

She shivered and screwed her fingers more tightly around the wheel. She wished she could start the engine and press her foot hard on the tiny accelerator – that she could send the car leaping forward, away and away from the great, flat expanse of barren land. But she could not do that because he was not with her, and without him there was no purpose, no journey to make.

She turned her ear to the open window. She did not look upwards, for she could hear clearly enough the sound of the engine. It was a sound that changed with infinite variations as the plane climbed and climbed. She saw, without looking, that the plane was growing smaller with each spiral. She tried to imagine him sitting there, his strong, thick-veined hands firmly around the joystick, his leather-coated figure fitting into its allotted space in the beloved machine. It was something she could only imagine, for she had never seen him like that. She wished to do so, she wished to be part of him, wearing the same coat, sitting in the same seat; to be with him high up in the clouds, anywhere ... She wished only to be with her love. But he had decreed no, with unusual firmness, and she had never crossed the outer edges of the aerodrome. Instead, she drove the silent coupe as near as she dared and then sat in it silently, white face and white hands, not unlike a ghost, listening.

She turned her head restlessly and saw, advancing across the wide airfield like a fly across a bare ceiling, the hatless, dishevelled figure of Manning. He was plump and round, bald-headed, blind in the left eye, asthmatic, a chain-smoker, irritable and self-opinionated, a mechanical genius, and the only other person in the world whose love for Royce, she acknowledged, matched her own. And of this she was fearful, for though it was to her that Royce came for his oblivion, it was with Manning that he experienced his achievement and ambitions.

Manning climbed through a gap in the hedge, puffing and blowing.

'I thought I'd find you here,' he said. 'Did you see that take-off?'

'Yes.'

'It was a darling. Just like out of a text-book. Darley was impressed.'

'Who's Darley?'

'From RAF. There's several of them come down specially. They're over at the clubhouse. Would you like to come and meet them?'

She shook her head.

'Okay.' Manning hesitated. She felt his bright little eyes examining her shrewdly. As he might examine a blueprint, she thought resentfully.

'Do you mind if I sit in the car for a while, then?'

'No, of course not.' She smiled, and flipped open the door. Manning heaved his large person into the spare seat and closed the door carefully. She was conscious of him beside her, shifting about like a restless sea, moving first one leg and then the other, leaning back against the seat and then twisting himself into another position. She shot a glance at him and saw his fingers along the window sill, drumming out some senseless pattern. He is in a state, she thought, with a flash of pity. She wondered if he was strung up about the plane or about Royce. Both, she supposed. It was, after all, almost impossible to differentiate between the two.

Something of Manning's nervous tension communicated itself to her. She produced a silver cigarette case from her handbag and flicked it open.

'Thanks,' said Manning. He lit a match. 'You keeping me company?'

'Yes. I can do with one.'

'Uhuh.' He did not seem to be conscious of her own strain, or if he was did not reveal it. When he had lit both their cigarettes he held the match between the nicotine-stained tips of his finger and thumb and watched it curiously, until Mathilde gave a sharp cry of warning. He laughed and threw the match out of the window.

'I had the situation in control,' he said. He took a long puff at the cigarette and then leaned back, exhaling the smoke into a slow spiral. But she could feel him, all the time, listening to the faraway buzz of the engine.

'How long will it last?' she asked.

'Oh, well, this time not long. Another ten minutes, perhaps. Then, of course, he may decide to have another shot.'

She was silent.

'It's quite customary,' he went on reassuringly. 'It will give him a chance to check up on his first assessments. But it won't take so long the second time.'

He eyed her curiously, a trifle impatiently.

'After all, he's been on hundreds of test flights before. He's a wonderful pilot. It's child's play to him. I remember – ' He silenced himself abruptly.

'*You* remember,' she said, as if taunting herself. 'Yes. You will have more to remember. You've been with him. You've shared all his adventures.'

'Not all,' he reminded her patiently. 'Most, but not all. Johnny was flying some years before I met him.'

'Yes. Where was it – some flying circus, wasn't it?'

'That's right. He used to tour the country, he and a friend. They'd pitch camp on the outskirts of a different town each day and take people for joy rides at five shillings a time. Ten shillings to include stunting. You know,' said Manning with a grin, 'I can just imagine Johnny at that. He must have loved it.'

'Yes,' she said. 'I expect he did. It was sort of – free, I suppose.'

'That's it.'

'What happened, then?'

Manning flicked some ash off his cigarette.

'Well ... the friend got killed. One of those things. The plane was wrecked. Royce was at a loose end. He got a job instructing somewhere. That's how I met him. Quite casually, through another pilot. In a pub.'

'Funny,' murmured Mathilde. 'Funny. I met him in a pub.'

'Oh, yes?' said Manning, his mind faraway. 'We were interested in each other at once. I had all the mechanical knowledge but I hadn't got the flying experience – or the flying instinct, you might say. He had that.'

'It's his everything.'

'In a way. It was funny how neatly we fitted in. I mean about the plane. The idea of it, and the building of it.'

'It's taken a long time,' she said, with a flicker of irony.

'Has it?' He seemed genuinely surprised. She knew that it must be at least six years since they began. Six years ago she had not even known Royce, but already Manning had been his friend. It was ironic, she supposed, that her jealousy should be focused on another man – and a white monoplane.

'Somehow I always feel as if it's his plane,' said Manning. It was as if he had read her thoughts. 'The design's mine all right, the engineering and the technical construction are all out of my brain – and yet, somehow it's his. It's as if – ' He scratched his shining bald head, perplexedly searching for the right words. ' – as if I'd made a human body, but he supplied the blood.'

'The soul, perhaps you mean?'

He shrugged.

'As you will. I'm not a religious man myself.'

She had to smile at that, knowing that he was essentially a good man and more religious than most who would profess to be so.

'I mean what I say,' he said, misunderstanding her smile. 'The plane is his. Surely you must have – sensed that. Look at the time he's spent with it. The way he looks at it even.'

'You forget,' she said dully, 'I have never been with him and the plane. The plane – ' she tried not to sound spiteful – ' – comes first.'

'Well, it's natural just now, isn't it?' Manning pondered. 'In that case, then, you wouldn't have seen how he went on the afternoon he first took it up.'

'I didn't know – what afternoon?' she said sharply, her mind fastening on to the new hurt like a leach. 'I thought this was the first flight.'

'Oh. I suppose he hadn't mentioned it. Damn!' said Manning. 'For God's sake don't say I let it out. It was last Thursday. Quite safe. The plane had been ready several days, just waiting for a new hood. He only took her up a few minutes. Said he couldn't resist it any longer. You can understand, after all this time. She flew like a bird ... And after all,' he stumbled on, seeing the frown still dark on her face, 'It was a practice for today. Just as well, with all these big-wigs coming.'

But she was not listening to him. She was remembering the Thursday. They had met in the morning, as usual. He always picked her up on the way to the aircraft works. She had noticed a certain restlessness about him that she could not quite define. When he turned the car away from London and out to the country she was surprised, but pleased. They drove for an hour, almost in silence, glorying in the sunshine and the escape. They stopped by a lake not far off the Guildford bypass. There was not a ripple disturbing the surface. The only other sign of human life was an old man fishing in the far corner. He seemed to have fallen asleep; his line dangled gently in the breeze, uncaring. It was the sort of time when there were no cares. They sat there against a fallen pine tree, basking in the sunshine, and she thought it was perhaps one of their happiest times. When, after lunch at a nearby pub, he suddenly looked at his watch and said he had forgotten an important appointment and he must tear away – would she mind if he put her on a train at the nearest station? – she had not minded. It had seemed as well to end something perfect, rather than to overstay it.

Now she understood. All the time his mind had only been half with her. Half of it had been contemplating the plane, enraptured with it – until at last, the call had been too great.

She stubbed her cigarette against the chrome edge of the dashboard. She felt like weeping, like forsaking the struggle. In that moment, if he had been there, she would have given up all pretences, would have thrown her arms round him, closing them like prison gates – if only it would have possessed him to her completely.

But he was not there.

Alarmed out of herself she listened.

'Manning,' she said tremulously. 'The plane. I can't hear it.'

'Of course not,' he said easily. 'It will be out of hearing by now.'

He lit a fresh cigarette. He was thinking about the plane he had built. He was remembering the first evocative, dubious lines he had drawn with a stubble of blue pencil and a sheet torn out of a 3d. notebook. They had been sitting in a corner of the saloon bar. Royce's drink had splashed on the table, and part of the notebook was stained with beer. 'Don't mind that,' Royce had laughed. 'Nothing can stop us now. One day that plane will be flying high – higher than any other, mark my words.' And now the words had come true. They were Royce's words, but they were his, Manning's ideas. They were Royce's eyes that lit up, but they were Manning's neat hands that drew the specifications. They were Royce's laughter and life that made them carry on in the face of all difficulties, but they were Manning's speculative mathematics that produced the inverse ratio and the aileron strain. And yet – it was *Royce's* plane now, up there, hidden in the clouds. That was the truth.

I suppose I ought to be jealous, Manning thought curiously. Deep down he knew that he was.

'I still think we ought to hear *something*,' said Mathilde irrationally.

They sat there in silence, listening. After a while she brought out the cigarettes again. They lit up, and Manning flipped the match out of the window. This time it was still lit when it fell on the ground. For a moment the flame caught a blade of grass and flamed up, then it died into black dust.

They both watched it, with curious intenseness. Then, with a sigh, they sank back into their seats and watched the blank afternoon sky.

Royce began to climb the plane above the lower clouds, tugging persistently at the joystick, watching the shape of the fuselage against the blue background of the sky. He guided the plane round in sweeping circles, the rambling green contours of the earth slowly fading and merging into great hazy ripples, darkening in the late sunlight. He glanced continually at the indicator figure, quivering phosphorescently in front of him. He watched with approval its steady rise. Two thousand ... three thousand ... four thousand ... five thousand ... six thousand ... seven thousand ... He concentrated entirely on the climb, following the same pattern of movements – pushing the throttle well forward, jerking slightly at the joystick, easing the rudder-bar down to the left – easing it all the time, gently and delicately – absorbing, comfortingly, the rich throbbing of the powerful engine.

I *know* this plane, he thought, and as the thought passed through him his hands instinctively reached forward to touch, with familiar movements, the surrounding instruments and background. For he knew, also, that there could never be anything else in his life so familiar and known. Although he was ensconced in the closed cockpit, shut into a world of his own, he had little difficulty in seeing the whole of the white monoplane in his imagination, watching it, as if through the eyes of some detached observer, as it slid upon its virgin path. He saw each wing, cut to a fine tapering finish, balanced perfectly – as perfectly, he would swear, as the most lovely bird's wings. He saw the pointed nose glittering when the sunshine caught it, glittering like an enormous eye that saw all, that penetrated to the darkest corner. He saw the short, stubby body that yet had a curious grace about it, that curved into a neat fan reminding him of some delicate fish. And he felt running through it all – the wings and the body and the great eye, himself engraved into his pattern in the cockpit – the motion of the engine, the relentless purring thunder that was symbolised by the threshing of the propeller. He sat there and saw the plane as a thing of beauty, impelled by some irresistible power upwards and onwards, and he was excited and uplifted and impelled himself.

Eight thousand ... nine thousand ... ten thousand ... He passed through clouds that swirled around him in great white blobs, oozing and spreading like ethereal pools of water. Sometimes the sunshine came dancing through the clouds, lighting them up into a fantastic fairy webbing, coloured a thousand shades and tints. He drove the plane onwards, its screaming propeller slicing a white-shrouded pathway. Soon, with that startling surprise which had always been one of the thrills of his life, he climbed right out of the clouds, entering a dream world. As the clouds fell away, blanketing the earth with their huge snowy waves, he found himself alone in the void of the sky – the whole horizon shimmering with gold and red. Ahead of him, far across the top of the clouds, he could now see the unshadowed sun, still pouring out its weeping warmth.

Fifteen thousand ... sixteen thousand ... seventeen thousand ... eighteen thousand ... He began to adjust his oxygen apparatus, tightening his helmet, pressing the thick woollen gloves hard on to his hands. He stared at the indicator stoically. Nineteen thousand ... twenty thousand ... He had never been higher than this but he never doubted the plane would do it. It was curious, he had almost lost the ability to feel any concern of a material kind. He was touched by a fleeting thought, grasping at something that seemed far out of his comprehension – back there, on the ground, on that strange other land. People, faces, problems. He felt he ought, in some way, to be conscious of them. But he found them eluding his grasp, and he knew that he was deliberately shelving them. He knew that, in any case, it was too late. He was part of the plane and the plane was climbing, like a great bird, to its freedom.

Twenty-one thousand ... As the finger quivered on the mark he laughed nervously, aware of a new, almost painful tension. The climbing was slower now, more difficult in the rarefied air. The strain of forcing the plane on, lifting it up through an atmosphere almost too slight to bear it, began to press achingly into his fingers and his arms, into the muscles of his legs. Twenty-two thousand ... twenty-three thousand ... He watched the bright nose of the plane – rising, rising, rising; curving, curving, curving; rising and curving and rising and curving and rising and curving. Twenty-four thousand ... He mumbled a tuneless refrain into his mouthpiece, narrowing his eyes to slits, willing himself and the plane upwards and upwards. The breath hissed slowly out between his teeth. He felt an itching at the back of his throat. He gave a last desperate heave at the joystick. He felt it was momentous, a test not only of the plane and of him, but of the two of them as one, as a unit – a test of the strength of what bound them together. And he knew it would be the glory of his life, because he was reaching out beyond whatever he had known.

'One spade,' said Mrs Royce.

'Pass,' said Miss Angel. She gave a mock shudder. 'I hope you haven't got that horrid ace, anyway. It always gives me the creeps.'

'I'm inclined to agree with you,' said Mrs Elmers, poker-faced. 'Two spades, partner.'

'Two no trumps,' said Mr Armitage. 'Two no trumps, I say, Miss Angel,' he repeated, fixing a disapproving eye on his partner.

'Oh, I hear you Mr Armitage,' simpered Miss Angel.

'Three spades,' said Mrs Royce. She shrugged her elegant, slightly too thin shoulders. 'A lot of superstitious nonsense if you ask me, Miss Angel.'

She looked at her cards. The ace of spades was four from the left. It seemed to her to symbolise not 'the creeps' but a sense of power. She knew, irrevocably, that it would make its trick. Perhaps, with some finessing, more than one trick. She had an astute, mathematical mind. She began reckoning and counting, while her partner laid down her hand. She counted with the fingers of one hand, almost imperceptibly. They were long, polished fingers, with bright red nails that shone in the electric light. The nails were over long, but brittle. Sometimes she broke one and it worried her endlessly.

'That's a nice blouse you've got on, Mrs Royce,' said Mrs Elmers.

'Oh, d'you think so? I'm *so* glad. I wasn't quite sure.'

She ran a finger down the edge of it, caressingly. Her face was quite animated.

'It's such a relief to get an outside opinion. One likes to have one's ideas confirmed.'

'Well, I'm sure I like it very much,' said Mrs Elmers firmly. She was a firm, solid woman, in everything she did and was. An excellent companion at bridge.

'So do I,' said Miss Angel quickly. 'What does your husband think of it, Mrs Royce?'

'Oh, him,' said Mrs Royce. 'He never notices anything.'

'I haven't had the pleasure of seeing Mr Royce, lately,' said Mr Armitage. 'Is he very busy?'

'I suppose so,' said Mrs Royce carelessly. She pulled in her fifth trick and led a small trump, with infinite calculation. 'He's always busy. It does make things rather difficult sometimes,' she said, her voice taking on a subtle inflection of righteous injury. 'I mean there are so many things about a house that need a man's attention. Bills and things. I had to sack the gardener yesterday. I don't know how I'll get a new one. Johnny ought to see to things like that, really. Now there's something wrong with the telephone. And then there – Ah, my trick, I see.'

She smiled, for a moment forgetting her process of complaints.

'Well, if I can help – ' began Mr Armitage, coughing.

Mrs Royce did not hear him. She was running the tip of her tongue along her upper lip. She was wondering if she could now finesse her jack. She was quite tense with the excitement.

'Your dummy's lead, Mrs Royce,' said Miss Angel.

She led the jack from dummy. Mr Armitage hesitated imperceptibly, and played under. She played a low one herself. Miss Angel grimaced and put down a three of spades.

'Ooh, la-la!' exclaimed Mrs Royce. 'One I never expected.'

'Now, now, Mrs Royce, you knew very well,' said Mrs Elmers with mock indignation.

'No, really. Well ... And I think the last two are mine. Ace and king of trumps.'

She laid down the remainder of her hand with a gesture in which there was just the faintest touch of the dramatic. She enjoyed such moments hugely. She felt herself the focus of their attention, the successful one, the lady on whom luck smiled. She always remembered with great pleasure the afternoon she won the jackpot on the fruit machine. She had talked about it for days afterwards. The others had been tickled pink. Not Johnny, of course. Not him. He didn't seem a bit interested at all.

As she thought of him, momentarily, her mouth tightened. He had no consideration for her feelings. The other night she had specially wanted him to come to dinner with her at the Harveys. It was so awkward being the unaccompanied woman. It seemed to throw things out of balance. But of course he wouldn't come. She did think he might have thought about that aspect of it. Of course, she'd been hurt, *terribly hurt*. But she hadn't said a word. And what's more, she hadn't let it get her into one of her moods, as she could quite justifiably have done. No, she'd been perfectly friendly and cheerful to Johnny. She'd told him all about the afternoon bridge party, and given him the gossip about Mrs Barnes, and what Mr Armitage had said about the Government. She'd shown him the new hat she'd bought that morning in the West End – perfectly sweet little thing it was, and suited her hair-style admirably. The assistant had been quite loquacious.

But not Johnny. No, not Johnny. He wasn't a bit interested. In fact he had seemed quite preoccupied about something or other. She shrugged her slim shoulders. He was always preoccupied about something or other. It was too bad he didn't spare a little time and thought for his wife. It really was.

She gathered the cards together.

'My shuffle, I think.'

'Correct,' said Mr Armitage, with a wink.

She shuffled and dealt. The cards went round smoothly in their clock-wise circle. The white elegant hand with the carefully polished finger nails slid round and round, at each destination giving an expert flick of a card. It was a hand complete in itself, that could carry out adequately a certain number of movements within a limited sphere – and was incapable of venturing beyond.

She came to the end of the pack. The last four cards fluttered down, like leaves from a tree. The last one was her own. She turned up the tip of the corner. It was the ace of spades.

She pulled her cards together and began sorting them out. I wonder what on earth he was so preoccupied about, she thought vaguely. And then, seeing with a rush of pleasure that she had king queen jack four times in diamonds, she forgot about everything else.

'Your bid, Miss Angel,' she said jovially.

The indicator figure quivered wildly then stuck: *twenty-five thousand feet*. He held the plane there, circling round in a faltering circle. Looking out through the frosted windscreen he saw the indescribable measurement of his triumph – a dream world of inscrutable blue, a lake of indigo waters. Sitting upright in his cockpit it seemed to him that his eyes were suddenly cleansed, suddenly alive as with a piercing new vision. So that now, alone in his life, he could even see beyond the blueness to where strange restless shadows marked the boundaries of the whole universe ... The wonder of it flooded over him, filling him with a surge of power that carried him into mystic communion with the sense of beauty around him, poising him on a pinnacle of eternity. The moment of truth, delicate and transient, like the raindrop holding all in its fleeting rainbow ... He saw himself as a ghostly rider and the monoplane as his white horse, riding out of the darkness into the light. He knew then he could never go back.

He raised his hands, involuntarily, in the moment of wonder, his eyes turned upward. Then the plane's nose faltered and plunged downwards, falling, falling, falling ... falling into space with a single frightening whine.

He bent forward in the cockpit, feeling no fear, only a supreme exhilaration. Conscious of an all-embracing freedom, he fought the more savagely for mastery of the plane – clutching at the joystick, heaving against the wild gusts of air that tore at the bowels of the plane and tried to whirl it into a vortex.

The plane whined down and down. He crouched deep into the dark interior, aware of the strange heavy weight of his falling body – aware, and yet careless, of the pain growing upon him sweetly – finally engulfing him into its vast drowning sea. He felt the perspiration seeping out of his skin – felt from afar the strange pumping of blood, the flushing of his cheeks, a hot line throbbing across his forehead. The sudden stabs of pain seared into his neck, his shoulders, his back, into his whole trembling body. Before his surprised eyes, the shadows in the cockpit began to move, writhing and twisting into tantalising shapes. They began swaying towards him and away again, leaving him drenched in sweat. He wanted to cry out, but his tongue filled his mouth, smothering his voice. He felt a great weight pulling him forward, pressing him down and down and down ... He looked at his hands, and they were no longer a part of him, but detached and unreal.

Unemotionally, he saw that they were quivering, rubber-like, as they clasped the joystick.

Then his hands dropped. The plane lurched forward; poised like a great lop-sided boulder on a cliff; then began falling forward, turning over and over, and round and round – flashing through the dying rays of sunshine like a silver spinning-top. The movement caught him up, a piece of ballast, tossing him up and down and banging his limbs against the sides of the cockpit – tearing a great rent across his flying coat. He felt the crackle of thin flesh and bone against a steel frame, saw blood spurt across his hand. In desperation he managed to get a grip on the control board, to drag himself back into the seat. Then another lurching movement hurled him away, sending him crashing against the windscreen.

He lay there soft and crumpled, warm with pain. His eyes, only his eyes, remained restless, darting one way and the other for the way of escape. But at last they flickered into two silent pools, and giving himself drunkenly up to the tremendous relief of surrender, he let himself spin away and away, a part of the silver streaming aeroplane. Now there were no more burdens, no more struggles, now there was only a single silver bird diving triumphantly out of the sky; diving, diving, diving ...

Edward Royce, riding home from school on his new bicycle, aimed for a gap in the traffic that was not there, then jammed on his brakes.

'Look where you're going, son,' grumbled the bus driver.

He mumbled some apology, resting for a minute with one foot on the curb. He could feel his heart pounding. The huge red-bus had practically shaved the hair off the side of his head. His eyes, that were in any case round and large, grew more so as he contemplated, with an intensity of gory detail, what might have happened to him if ... He saw himself lying stretched on the pavement, the crowd gathering round, someone shouting 'Give him air' – the clanging of the ambulance bell, the crowd parting, uniformed men approaching with a stretcher – their concerned, grave faces and the significant look passing between them – that he would accidentally glimpse through half-dazed eyes), the look that meant it was a matter of hours, minutes perhaps.

Still fascinated with his own fantasies, he rode on along the big arterial road with its flat, identical looking rows of houses and gardens. Then, coming to the traffic lights he turned left and free-wheeled down the long slow hill towards the river.

By now, in his mind, he was in hospital, surrounded by screens, white-clad nurses tiptoeing about. He supposed they would come and ask him if he would like to send for someone. Yes, they always did that. And he would say – ? He frowned. Well, he supposed ... Best of all, of course, he'd like to have Fisher there. Fisher was fun, you didn't have to dress up and parade about with Fisher, you could be yourself. He and Fisher ran a secret society of their own. They worked out its campaigns as they cycled to and fro from school each day – only today Fisher had gone to the dentist and half the society had to make the journey on its own. Yes, if he was dying in hospital he'd like Fisher to come and tell him the latest news. Although, if he *really* was dying ... Well, weren't you supposed to send for your mother or something?

He grimaced, swinging the bicycle around a corner and down the last part of the incline. His mother would want to dress him up in his best pyjamas. You can't die looking untidy, she'd say. Gosh, that's rather witty, he thought, and broke into a broad smile. He'd tell that to Fisher. Actually now, Fisher's mother was a grand sort. She let them play football in the spare room and even played table tennis with them herself.

As he came level with the river and began riding along the towpath, he saw the small speck of a plane on the horizon, climbing higher and higher until it disappeared into the clouds. He wondered if it might by any chance be his father. It gave him a queer feeling to think, for that moment, of his own father miles and miles away up there in the air – and him down here. In an odd way it gave him a more real conception of his father than he ever had when they were in the same room.

Well, now, perhaps he would have his father and not his mother to the bedside? He played with the thought, conscious at once of a curious relief from the previous thought. And then his mind went to the breakfasts, almost the only time when he saw his father, and how the two of them would sit there in long awkward silences, so that he never really enjoyed his breakfast until his father inevitably got up and said, 'Well, I must be off now, son,' and went through the dining-room door. His mother was never there, of course. She had breakfast in bed. He wished his father would have breakfast in bed as well, and he could have his in peace. Still, he didn't know, from what he's observed he didn't really blame his father for preferring not to have breakfast in bed with mother. She was rather sharp first thing in the morning.

He got off his bike and went and sat on the edge of the towpath opposite a weir. It was his favourite spot. A series of wooden posts stretched across the river and between them the water plunged into frothing waterfalls. You could just stare at the water and watch its white-plumed dive going on endlessly, for ever and ever and ever, it seemed.

He wondered if his father had come and sat here when he was a boy. No, of course, he wouldn't, he had lived in some other part. But wherever he had lived, he probably had done something like this. It was funny to think of his father as a little boy. But at least you could imagine it. Now you couldn't think of mother as a little girl. No, it was impossible. As he tried to do so his mouth curled a little in quiet derision.

He wished Fisher were here. They could evolve a scheme for crossing the river and boarding that derelict houseboat. At least, it looked derelict. You never could be sure. He read a story once about a sinister crook who hid for a year on a houseboat and murdered people. Fisher would like that. He thought with affection of Fisher now sitting in the dentist's chair. Poor old Fisher, bet he was hating it. Touched, he said to himself, I hope old Fisher doesn't have too bad a time.

He looked at the water again, swishing over and down, over and down. Funny thing water. He preferred it to the sky. You could touch water, you couldn't touch anything in the sky. He knew because he had been up in an aeroplane. It was one of his great trump cards over Fisher. 'My father took me up for a ride in his aeroplane.' But he hadn't wanted to go again. No, he's been quite sure about that. There were times when he had felt quite sick. And, besides, it wasn't all that fun. Not half such fun as riding in a sports car along the by-pass. Now, that *was* something. When he'd tried to explain this, his father had smiled curiously. But all the same he'd been disappointed, you could sense that.

It was curious thinking about his father like that. He hadn't meant to. He hardly knew his father. He seemed to spend all his time, weekends as well, at work. And before that he had been away abroad, teaching flying. It must be fun to go abroad. Sail across the seas, explore strange lands. He and Fisher were going to go abroad. They were planning it now. They were going to save up and buy a canoe, and then set off. There was a chap who'd crossed the Atlantic in a canoe. It was easy really. And you carried the canoe over your heads when you wanted to go across land.

He stirred irritably. He'd have to be getting on soon. He supposed his mother would have the bridge people in. He'd be expected to go and wash and put on some clean clothes and present himself. And everyone would be expected to say polite things, including himself.

Wouldn't old Fisher laugh if he could see it! He frowned. Jolly good job he couldn't. He'd never taken Fisher home and he never would. You couldn't explain it to Fisher. He wouldn't understand. Perhaps now, if his father was there ... He remembered an occasion when his father *had* been home, unexpectedly. It had been strange, disturbing, to see his father home in the daytime. He had watched him, through a window, pottering about in the garden. At last timidly, he had gone down and walked over to where, he discovered, his father was building a little rockery.

After a time Edward offered to help. His father seemed to become aware of his presence for the first time. His face lit up – he had keen blue eyes that were warm and friendly, and that Edward hardly ever saw.

'Of course, of course. You'll be a great help,' he said.

And so they worked together, side by side on the path. Edward assembled the little, odd-shaped flints and stones and his father shovelled the earth into place. They worked steadily, without speaking much, and gradually the fruits of their labour emerged in the shape of a speckled rectangular rockery.

'That's fine, father,' he said, standing up and admiring it. And he felt a curious comradeship between them.

'Not bad, eh?' His father, too, stood back. Then he frowned and pointed. 'Don't you think perhaps ... if we made a grand pinnacle?'

Edward couldn't see that it was terribly important. But his father bent down and built up the flints to a tiny pinnacle, with infinite, almost loving care. He went on and on until eventually he tried to perch one tiny flint on the very top.

'It's no good, father,' he said. 'It can't be done.'

'Oh, I don't know,' his father said, staring at the rockery with a curious dreaminess. 'I think it can.' And sure enough the next attempt secured the flint at the top, like a triumphant white flag.

'There!' his father said, and this time when he stood back his face was filled with a smile, and he looked curiously happy.

Edward was happy, too, but not quite so happy as when they were working together building the rockery up, step by step. It was as if the impulse in his father that made him build the last pinnacle had subtly set him apart. Edward would have been happier if there had been just the single, shared experiences. But he would have been happy either way if at least his father had come again the next afternoon and they had built another rockery, or perhaps planted a fruit tree, or mowed the lawn. As he lay in bed that evening a whole pattern of possible projects unravelled before his eyes. But the next day his father was at work again, and the next day, and, it seemed, all days after that. In the wet weather the rockery gradually crumbled away ...

Gosh, he thought, I've been staring at the water and daydreaming, and it's terribly late. I must hurry. And he fixed on his cycling clips and got his bicycle down from where it was leaning against the hedge.

As he wheeled it forward, preparatory to mounting, he thought for a moment his eye caught another speck in the sky — a speck that seemed to flash across the whole of his vision in a swift, final movement. He brushed his eye-lids with his fingers and blinked, thinking it was probably a fly. But it reminded him yet again of his father, and he had a curious conviction that it *was* his father he had seen flying in that aeroplane, earlier in the afternoon.

He mounted his bicycle and began riding along the rough towpath, abreast with the river, swirling to its endless horizon. I know what, Edward thought, I'll ask father tonight. That's it. I'll stay awake specially and I'll ask him if it was him flying. I'll ask him what it was like. Gosh, it must be strange to go up and up and up. Father must have had some wonderful experiences.

Suddenly he had again that sense of momentary comradeship with his father, suddenly he was sharing something with his father.

That's it, he thought. I'll ask him tonight, and he can tell me all about it. And he cycled home quickly, bending his head low and listening to the hum of the wet wheels on the tarred road, caught up in a sense of exhilaration and impending revelation.

The plane dived on, the wailing music of the engine rising and drowning Royce's senses. Drowsily he felt for the joystick, remembering some old instruction drilled into him. He made to pull the stick back, half expecting to feel the triumphant beat of the wings against the howling wind as they flattened out and soared up again into the sky. But the stick began flapping to and fro, and danced out of his grasp. For a moment, he looked out and saw white streams of mist billowing towards him like falling sheets of snow. Long ribbons of rainbow colours flashed in and out of his life; he saw, faraway, white waves and wet sands, and summer flowers along the tarmac path of the airfield.

Then, out of round luminous eyes he saw the bright beady eye of the setting sun winking at him, beckoning him home. With a tiny sigh he let himself sink deep down into the warm endless embrace of his mother-earth, the evening shadows slanting like rainbows across her soft grey-green breasts.